SHERLOCK HOLMES
and the
BAKER STREET IRREGULARS

CASEBOOK N⚬. 4

THE FINAL MEETING

TRACY MACK & MICHAEL CITRIN

ORCHARD BOOKS
An Imprint of
SCHOLASTIC INC.

New York Toronto London Auckland
Sydney Mexico City New Delhi Hong Kong

For Sadie May Citrin

Of the many sources we consulted,
the following were particularly helpful:
The Annotated Sherlock Holmes by Sir Arthur Conan Doyle, edited by
William S. Baring-Gould; *The New Annotated Sherlock Holmes* by Sir Arthur
Conan Doyle, edited by Leslie S. Klinger; *London Characters and Crooks*
by Henry Mayhew; *What Jane Austen Ate and Charles Dickens Knew*
by Daniel Pool; *The Victorian Underworld* by Kellow Chesney;
Bob's Your Uncle: A Dictionary of Slang for British Mystery Fans
by Jann Turner-Lord; and *Passenger Trains* by Christopher Chant,
edited by John Moore.

Lines 8–13 and 20–21 on page 5 are transcribed directly from
"The Adventure of the Final Problem" by Sir Arthur Conan Doyle.

ISBN 978-0-439-83672-2

10 9 8 7 6 5 4 3 2 1   10 11 12 13 14
Printed in the U.S.A. 40
First edition, July 2010
Book design by Steve Scott

"I tell you, Watson, in all seriousness, that if I could beat that man, if I could free society of him, I should feel that my own career had reached its summit, and I should be prepared to turn to some more placid line in life."

— "The Adventure of the Final Problem"

— • PREFACE • —

IN WHICH
THE END IS NEAR

Esteemed Reader,

For three volumes, I have faithfully shared
the adventures of the Baker Street Irregulars, the
devoted assistants to master detective Sherlock
Holmes, because, over time, scholars and
historians have failed to give them proper credit.

But by now, you know all this. So I will spare
you a lengthy introduction. I have neither the
inclination nor the fortitude for such formalities
anyhow. The proper thing to do, faithful reader, is
bid you farewell. Alas, I do so with a heavy heart.
Whether from sentimentality or melancholy, I
cannot say. But this shall be the last adventure

I tell — the gravest yet for our intrepid friends. I have asked myself countless times in the intervening years since *The Final Meeting*, could things ever again have been the same for the Irregulars? Oh, how fate has played with all of us!

Forgive me. I am blathering on when I said I would not. Come. As Master says, "The game is afoot."

Yours anonymously,
London, England
1955

CHAPTER ONE

THE FIRST MEETING

In the heart of London's West End, on a walkway across from 221B Baker Street, a skinny boy called Ozzie sat beside an upturned hat, looking mournfully into the eyes of passersby. Beside him, his best mate, Wiggins, belted out a tune with false enthusiasm.

> *"Now I am bound to the Spanish shore,*
> *Where thundering cannons loud do roar,*
> *Crown my desire, fulfill my wish,*
> *A pretty girl and a jug of this."*

Though it was late April, the chilly, damp air barely hinted of spring. Only the wind, with its faint scent of magnolia blossoms, suggested a change of season. Ozzie shivered in his thin coat and summoned a cough as Wiggins leaned over to check the bowler. Still only two pence. The strollers were not in a generous mood today.

> *"When I am dead and in my grave,*
> *And all my sorrows are past and fled,*
> *Crown my desire, fulfill my wish,*
> *Place on my tomb, a jug of this."*

Spiritlessly, he sang one last verse before sinking to the walkway beside Ozzie. "It's been weeks since Master beckoned us for a case. My voice is gone and we've almost no *bees and honey* to show for it." Wiggins shook his head. His stomach growled. "How's Master expect us to survive if he ain't payin' us? Soon we'll be back to roastin' rats."

Ozzie recoiled at the thought. "I'll eat spuds all day before I eat another rat. Too boney."

"Not if you have a nice fat one. You'll catch

us some fat ones, won't you, Shirley?" Wiggins scratched the back of his pet ferret, who lay curled in his lap.

"It has been too many weeks," Ozzie agreed. He looked up at the windows of Sherlock Holmes's flat. "No adventures, no mind work. I can't decide if Master has had no cases or is just handling them without us." The latter thought churned up a mass of feelings inside Ozzie, not the least of which being, Was Master avoiding *him* specifically?

Just then, the distinctive profile of Sherlock Holmes — tall and slim, with a prominent, beaklike nose — passed the second-floor window of his study. He was smoking his clay pipe and appeared deep in thought.

Ozzie sighed and removed a small volume from inside his coat pocket. "How about some practice, Wiggins?" He flipped a page and read the title, *"The Man in the Iron Mask."*

"Please, Oz, no readin' lessons now. Things are tough enough." Wiggins balled two fists in protest.

3

"But you're becoming quite good, mate. You recognize most words. In no time, you'll be reading the *Strand* all by yourself."

"I like learnin' the stories, Oz, and I don't mind the work of readin'. But speakin' the words aloud, well, it makes me feel like a *burke*."

"You won't feel simple if you learn to read, Wiggins."

As the two spoke, a large modified brougham pulled by two horses rolled down Baker Street and halted in front of 221B. The boys stood and watched a thin older man in a top hat and black overcoat exit the carriage.

Ozzie gasped when he turned in their direction. The domed forehead, sunken face, and deep reptilian eyes were unmistakable. The two locked eyes, and a snakelike smile spread across the man's thin lips before he strode casually into 221B.

Ozzie shuddered — not because the most dangerous man in all of England had fixed him with a hard stare. It was the familiarity of the gaze that unnerved him.

"That was Professor Moriarty!" exclaimed

Wiggins. "And he walked inside Master's building just like that — unannounced. It makes no sense."

Ozzie nodded his agreement. "Let's follow."

Cautiously, the boys crossed Baker Street and entered through the same door. They climbed the stairs. Stopping in the hallway, they listened to a conversation that had by now begun.

"All that I have to say has already crossed your mind," said Moriarty.

"Then possibly my answer has crossed yours," Holmes replied.

"You stand fast?"

"Absolutely," Holmes said without hesitation.

Wiggins concentrated as the two men conversed in some sort of code of unfinished sentences. Though the meaning of the actual words was not clear, he sensed the underlying message: Moriarty had had enough of Holmes's interference and was threatening him.

"You must drop it, Mr. Holmes," said Moriarty, "you really must." Ozzie's heart pounded. This is the end, he thought. They are done with each other. Moriarty has turned up without warning for the meeting before the final battle. He felt the oxygen empty from his lungs and quietly reached inside his coat for his cod liver oil tonic and took a swig.

When it was clear that the discussion had ended, Wiggins pulled Ozzie down the stairs and onto the street. As he did so, Moriarty's burly driver spun around, stepped off the brougham, and raised a fist in warning. He was about to give chase, but the boys fled down Baker Street, swift as rabbits.

CHAPTER TWO

AN ATTEMPT IS MADE ON HOLMES'S LIFE

Moments later, Ozzie and Wiggins peered anxiously around the corner of Dorset Street and watched Moriarty and his driver ride off. Relieved, they returned to the walkway across from Holmes's flat.

"Sounds like Master is in a heap of trouble." Wiggins's hazel eyes squinted with concern. In all the time he'd worked for Sherlock Holmes, he'd never imagined the great detective might need the gang's help for his *own* protection.

Ozzie agreed. "Moriarty will no longer tolerate Master foiling his plans. But there must be something more. Moriarty doesn't just show up and threaten. He sends others for that."

7

"What do you think is happenin'?"

Ozzie shook his head. "Master has planned something that endangers Moriarty. I'm just not sure what." He still felt rattled from seeing Holmes's archenemy. He recalled the underground dig of the Calico Finch case. After Moriarty had been discovered and fled through a tunnel, Ozzie had pursued him. Or had Moriarty summoned him? The details were foggy, but Ozzie understood that he had been drawn to the man for reasons he could not explain, even to himself. There was a strange warmth about Moriarty, almost a fatherliness, as he offered Ozzie the chance to join his organization. Wiggins had witnessed part of the encounter, and later, when he confronted Ozzie, he doubted his friend's loyalty. Ozzie knew that Wiggins had not understood what had happened. In truth, Ozzie still wondered. Did he *really* want to follow Moriarty? Would he have provided the care and attention that Holmes didn't seem capable of?

Wiggins watched his friend's expression. "You're thinkin' about him, aren't you?"

Ozzie scratched his head. "That whole exchange, Wiggins, it was . . . odd, it was . . . I wasn't myself."

Wiggins paused, but then smiled and shoved Ozzie's shoulder. "You're me ol' *china*."

Ozzie returned the push and smiled. Still, his friend's faith in him did not wash away the uneasy feeling that seeing Moriarty had churned up.

As the boys talked, a man with a military bearing paced down the walkway toward them. He wore tweed trousers and a matching coat with the cut of a hunter's garment. He looked like a country squire or a member of a gentleman's hunting party. Ozzie had seen such attire during his travels through Oxfordshire while searching for his great-aunt Agatha. Under his right arm, the man carried a long, narrow bolt of cloth tied at both ends with twine. He stopped at a door directly across the street from 221B, removed a key from his pocket, and entered the building.

The boys stared after him. Ozzie read the sign for a leasing agent posted on the second floor. "I've never seen that gent before. Maybe he recently rented the place."

"He wasn't dressed like a tailor. So why was he carrying a roll of cloth?" Wiggins asked.

"Good question, mate —" Before Ozzie could venture a guess, cinders fell from above and sprinkled the walkway around them.

Wiggins looked up. "He must have gone to the roof."

Ozzie checked the door. The man had neglected to lock it behind him. Quietly, Ozzie pushed it open. Seeing no one in the hallway, he signaled Wiggins to follow.

The boys crept silently up the stairs, peering around corners before they proceeded. There was no one in the stairway, and the doors on each floor were ajar, revealing empty rooms. On the landing of the top floor, a cast-iron ladder reached up through a door in the ceiling. The door had been left open. The boys could see the sky.

They stood quietly and listened, but heard nothing.

Ozzie placed his foot on the bottom rung and paused.

10

"You sure you're up for the climb, Oz?" Wiggins whispered. It was no secret that Ozzie had a fear of heights, which he'd discovered during the case of the Amazing Zalindas.

He nodded and climbed slowly. Wiggins followed.

Ozzie peeked out, but the hatch door blocked his view. All he could see was a brick wall about three feet high which appeared to circle the roof.

When they climbed out, they saw the man in tweed, crouched in a hunter's position, facing Holmes's flat. The cloth he'd been carrying lay unraveled on the roof. His arms held a long, thin rifle, which was aimed directly at the window of Holmes's study.

While Wiggins puzzled over what to do, Ozzie took four long steps, picked up the cloth, and threw it over the rifleman's head and face. Following his lead, Wiggins grabbed the twine and secured the cloth around the man's neck. Still grasping the rifle in one hand, the man attempted to yank off the cloth with the other. Ozzie and Wiggins held firm.

During the struggle, the rifle made a strange whooshing noise, followed by a sharp crack, before it fell to the roof.

Ozzie kicked it away as the man cursed and groped about wildly. The boys realized that they would not be able to subdue him, so they leapt back and fled through the hatch door and down the ladder.

As they exited the building and raced onto the walkway, they were met by Holmes, who ran at them from across the street. His smoking jacket remained neatly tied. He carried a pistol in his hand.

"Is the man with the air gun still in there?" he asked urgently.

Ozzie and Wiggins were slow to respond. Master had warned them repeatedly about putting themselves in harm's way.

"Answer me," Holmes demanded.

The boys nodded.

"I heard the bullet ricochet off the front of my building." Pushing past the boys, Holmes entered the building and sprang up the stairs. The boys followed. When they reached the roof, Holmes stood looking off the back side of the building as the man in tweed crept down the far end of the alley below and climbed into a waiting carriage. He carried a small roll of fabric in one hand.

Holmes turned to the boys. "I should lecture you for endangering yourselves, once again."

They shrunk beneath his hawklike stare.

"But then I would sound ungrateful to you for saving my life." Holmes gave them each an awkward pat on the shoulder.

"The man you attacked is Colonel Moran, a crack shot, the second most dangerous man in London — and Moriarty's closest associate. Few cross his path and survive. We were lucky this time."

Wiggins and Ozzie looked at each other, a little unnerved by Master's description.

Holmes turned and pocketed his gun. He bent down, picked up the discarded bullet shell, and held the canister under his nose. Holding it up, he observed, "This appears to be the shell from a handgun, not a rifle." His brow furrowed as he dropped down to examine the roof surface more closely.

"The professor has not waited long to fulfill his promise." Holmes stood and motioned to the boys to follow. "There are more details I must attend to in order to keep mine."

CHAPTER THREE

HOLMES SHARES
HIS PLAN

As Holmes paced the floor, Ozzie studied the contents of his sitting room: the rack of pipes on the mantle; the Persian slipper holding Master's strong-smelling pipe tobacco; an array of chemistry equipment, including test tubes, beakers, microscope, and burner; the gasogene and decanters; the *Encyclopædia Britannica*; Master's index of criminals, important people, and places; and the letters *V* and *R* that he had shot into the wall for target practice. By now, the place had a familiarity to Ozzie, though it did not feel like home.

Wiggins, on the other hand, could not take his eyes off Master's untouched breakfast: bacon, eggs, and blood pudding. How frustrating, thought Wiggins, that Master's landlady, Mrs. Hudson, prepares such fine meals, and they regularly go to waste.

"Wiggins, you and Osgood are welcome to my breakfast. I've no time for eating now." Holmes motioned to the silver platter, porcelain plates, and silverware resting on a fine white linen cloth before striding over to his desk and rummaging through the top drawer.

Eagerly, Wiggins sat down, skewered a slice of bacon, and ate it with small joyful bites. Hardly pausing to look up, he pointed to the platter and said, "Oz, come eat."

But Ozzie's mind was otherwise absorbed. Master *does* look like me, he thought as he studied the great detective.

Holmes stood tall and lean with a high forehead and narrow lips. Only my nose is quite a bit smaller, Ozzie noted. Could he be my father? Ozzie had not given up on the possibility. He had just lost the will to ask the question.

He thought about his trip to Oxfordshire. He'd never discussed with anyone what he'd learned there: that his great-aunt Agatha had kept pictures of Ozzie's mother and clippings about Holmes's early cases together in a trunk. And he'd never confided, even to Wiggins, that his mother had worked in Oxford during the same period that Holmes had studied there. Even though Master did not believe in coincidence, these two details — particularly when placed together and considered alongside the fact that Ozzie's mother had always been so secretive about his father — seemed too related to ignore.

When Ozzie had returned from his travels in the countryside, he showed the pictures of his mother to Holmes. But if the detective knew her, he had kept it to himself. Of course that was the trouble with all of this. Holmes was not a man to share his feelings. Ozzie sometimes wondered if he had any. Even if Ozzie mustered the courage to confront Holmes directly on the subject, he would likely say nothing or explain the illogical basis for such a presumption. The possibility of either of these responses was so painful that it paralyzed Ozzie. Perhaps he —

"Osgood, I am talking to you. Osgood?"

Holmes and Wiggins both stared at Ozzie as if he were an ill patient in a hospital bed.

"Are you with us, Osgood?" Holmes said sternly.

Ozzie nodded.

Wiggins resumed eating his breakfast.

"Very well," Holmes continued. "The time has come to put an end to Moriarty and his organization."

Ozzie sucked in his breath. Even Wiggins looked up and paused between bites.

"We have come up against Moriarty time and again. With each meeting, I have managed to foil his schemes. But alas, he always escapes only to return with a new plot more ingenious than the last. This pattern must end.

"For two fortnights, I have created an intricate web of such colossal proportion that it now permeates the full breadth of Moriarty's organization.

With confidence, I stand here and say that in three days, it will all be over — his entire organization will be brought to justice.

"Moriarty visited me today, and though his denials were strong, it was clear he knew the end was near."

So I was right, thought Ozzie.

Wiggins swallowed a mouthful of eggs. "What is going to 'appen?"

"For your own safety, you and the rest of the Irregulars must leave London. Moriarty will undoubtedly avenge his organization by attacking mine. I will make arrangements for you today." Holmes handed Ozzie an envelope filled with pound notes, several fivers, and a few tenners. Wiggins nearly choked. It was the most money he or Ozzie had ever seen, let alone held.

"Return to the carriage factory at once and wait for my direction. I will inform you of the plans shortly."

"But we want to help you, Master, like we always do," Wiggins said.

"You can assist me most by obeying my

instructions. Now if you will —" Holmes pointed to the door. "I assure you, we shall see each other again. Ready yourselves, and watch your step."

Leave London? Wiggins had not set foot outside the city in all of his twelve years. Where would they go? And how would he look after the gang in unfamiliar surroundings? Still, the serious expression on Master's face told Wiggins he had no choice but to listen. Before exiting the flat, he folded an egg and a slice of bacon inside a piece of toast and handed it to Ozzie, who, without thinking, stuffed it in his coat pocket.

As Ozzie took one last look around Master's study, he couldn't help but feel that he would not see it again for some time.

CHAPTER FOUR

TERROR AT
THE CASTLE

B ack at the Castle, the abandoned carriage factory that had been home to the gang ever since Wiggins discovered it several years ago, the nine other Irregulars lounged around the stone fire pit, roasting bits of potatoes on their cooking sticks.

Scavenged blankets, pillows, mats, and an assortment of bric-a-brac discovered on the street and in other places lay strewn about. A catwalk circled the upper perimeter of the large rectangular room, and a grand but damaged coach rested on blocks near the sealed front doors. Though the Grand Dame had been vandalized, the Irregulars were in the process of restoring her. The door had been fixed and reattached. The roughed-up exterior received a fresh coat of paint. And the seats had been reupholstered. Though the windows remained glassless and the old lady was sorely in need of further repairs, she still acted as a private place to lounge, play games, and act out adventures.

"These are rough times, boys. Not even a whole spud apiece," said Elliot as he studied the morsel on the end of his cooking stick. He was a stocky boy with bright red hair and a blazing temper to match. Though he had mellowed since he first joined the gang, he still had a knack for starting a fight. If not for his loyalty and his skills as a tailor — which kept the boys respectably clothed and their feet dry in shin-high leather moccasins — Wiggins might have tossed him out long ago.

"Aw, you know Wiggins won't let us starve, Stitch. Still, you could lose a little gut." Alfie laughed. He was the youngest Irregular, with white-blond hair that hung straight as straw and ears as big as wings.

"Don't bother me when I'm hungry, Elf. It'll be unpleasant for both of us." Elliot kept his voice even, but flashed a sharp stare and a yellow-toothed smile at Alfie, who turned his attention to his cooking stick and stifled himself. Scrappy as he was, he knew when *not* to annoy Elliot.

"Maybe Oz and Wiggins are scarin' up some work for us right now," he muttered.

"I miss workin' for Master. All we've done is lounge or wander about for weeks. It's like we've been *duckin' and divin'*. I been sweepin' the streets again, pushin' trash for less than pennies, but it's no life for me. And to think that my father wanted me to be apprenticed to a barrister." Rohan frowned.

"You should be a boxer," said Pete, who admired Rohan's strength. "You are big and you use your hands better than most blokes."

"Yeah, that would be smart: Rohan the Bombay Basher!" Fletcher stood and mimed a boxing stance.

"I'm from the East End," said Rohan, "not Bombay. And you know I don't like to fight."

The other boys ignored him.

"Rohan's our man."

"You could do it, mate. I've seen you knock down a bloke twice your size."

"We could make a load of *sugar and honey* bettin' on you."

"Ay, 'the Basher,' that's a good one."

Embarrassed, Rohan shook his head. "I told you, I'm no boxer."

The boys settled down.

"It's all right, Rohan," said Alfie. "You don't need to be no boxer. You can come mudlarkin' with me."

When the tide was out, Alfie loved to scavenge from the bottom of the River Thames. His treasures — old bottles cloudy with mud, an assortment of rusty tins and tools, a broken anchor, a carriage wheel — now decorated the Castle, even though Wiggins had warned him not to fill the place with junk that smelled like an old dock.

Rohan smiled and nodded to Alfie. In truth, the thought of wading out into the Thames gave him the *collywobbles*. His fisherman father had drowned at sea, and ever since, all bodies of water where the tide could rise up and snatch you made him uneasy and sad, all the more so knowing how much his father had loved the sea. The two of them used to take long walks along the river's edge just so he could be near water. Rohan's thoughts were occupied by memories when he smelled something strange. "What's that stench?" he asked the others.

"It's the fire pit," said Shem.

Rohan shook his head.

Noting his concern, Elliot stood, turned his head up toward the rafters, closed his eyes, and inhaled deeply through his nose. "I smell it, Rohan. What a *pen and ink*. It's like tar burnin'." An ill feeling wormed its way through his gut and into his throat, making him cough.

Elliot opened his eyes to discover that the roof was smoking in the back corner of the room. Images of his baby sister, wee Maureen, flashed across his mind. For a moment, he froze, recalling the fire that had claimed his whole family and their home. Elliot pointed to the ceiling. "Everyone up, the building is on fire!"

He and Rohan led the boys to the trapdoor. Elliot ran straight into it only to bounce back. He paused and gave it another push. "Bloody 'eck, it's stuck!" He looked back up at the ceiling. Flames were moving across two rafters.

In a rush, the boys kicked and heaved their weight against the door. Rohan rammed it with his shoulder. But it held fast.

"Can't we pry it open?" said James.

"There's nowhere for a bar to go," said Simpson.

"Don't we 'ave an axe or somethin'?" Fletcher said, knowing they didn't.

All the while, Elliot kept kicking the door as the carriage factory filled with smoke. "Any ideas, Ro?" he asked, his voice quavering. "Because we don't 'ave much time here."

Rohan followed his gaze, and the boys watched in horror as the flames spread from the back of the carriage factory toward them.

Rohan looked around. For all the tools and other things Alfie and the boys had collected, there was nothing that could help.

Just then, a beam at the rear of the factory sizzled and fell, crushing part of the catwalk on its descent. The flames swelled and licked at the floor and crept menacingly toward the boys. Some began to cough, others to cry.

Not knowing what else to do, Alfie left them and wandered over to the Grand Dame and climbed up. Calmly he laid back on the seat.

Rohan thought he was mad, until an idea struck him.

"Everyone to the Dame," he ordered. "Now!"

The boys did as they were told.

"Alfie, come down from there and help push."

Rohan stood behind the coach and gently rocked it on its support blocks. Alfie and Elliot quickly realized what he was doing. Alfie jumped down, and Elliot ordered everyone to help.

The boys thrust the coach forward and back.

"Careful," Rohan warned, "we want it to fall away from us, not on us."

With each push forward, the coach rocked toward the large front doors of the factory. With each rock back, the boys eased her so she would not topple off the blocks and crush them. Cinders rained down on their hair and in their eyes, but they persisted, pushing with more and more urgency. The coach swayed side to side, like a ship at sea.

Finally, the old lady heaved sideways, tilted off her base, and crashed through the front doors into the street, just as the roof of the carriage factory collapsed.

CHAPTER FIVE

SURVEILLANCE ON BAKER STREET

Meanwhile, Ozzie and Wiggins crouched behind a cart on Baker Street, discussing their meeting with Holmes. It was nearly eleven o'clock, and morning strollers began to fill the walkway. A chill wind bit into the boys' cheeks.

"Oz, he told us to return to the Castle."

"Someone tried to shoot him, Wiggins. We can't abandon him."

"Master can watch out for himself just fine. We need to help the others."

As the boys spoke, they noticed Pilar turn onto Baker Street.

Spotting them, she grinned and gave a jaunty wave.

29

"This ain't good timin'," Wiggins muttered.

Ozzie nodded. "Don't tell her that. Remember, she's one of us now."

After the gang had completed work on the Calico Finch case, Pilar was made an official member of the Baker Street Irregulars. Not only had her lip-reading skills proved invaluable in aiding Master and the gang at the perilous excavation site, but she'd reasoned convincingly with Wiggins that her cleverness in several prior cases had also been significant. Wiggins couldn't help but agree. And because the boys had been surprisingly open to the idea of letting a girl into the gang — most likely because it was Pilar, who knew how to get along with boys — they'd welcomed her with a feast and a ceremony. Pilar was sworn in by candlelight and promised to "go everywhere, see everything, and overhear everyone" in order to aid the good work of master detective Sherlock Holmes.

At the same time, Wiggins knew his gang and their personalities intimately. And Pilar could sometimes be pushy, especially when it came to doing the most important detective work, which was generally reserved for him and Ozzie. He took a breath and motioned for her to join them behind the cart.

"*Hola,*" Pilar sang as she approached. She wore her customary gray wool cape and silk head scarf. "Are you boys spying on Master?" Her emerald eyes twinkled.

Ozzie filled her in on the events of the morning.

"You mean I missed Professor Moriarty? *And* an attempt on Master's life?" Pilar frowned. She was lamenting her bad luck when Holmes exited 221B and turned in the direction of lower Baker Street.

"Do you think he saw us?" Pilar whispered.

"If he did," Ozzie noted, "he didn't stop to tell us not to follow."

Pilar smiled. "I like the way you think, Ozzie."

A bad feeling snaked through Wiggins's chest, from fear of Holmes's predicament or worry over the gang, he could not tell. "I really think we ought to return to the Castle. . . ."

"As soon as we find out where Master is going, we will, mate," Ozzie assured him.

Reluctantly, Wiggins agreed. Still, he could not shake the troubled feeling.

The three started a careful jog down Baker Street, pausing occasionally behind people, carriages, and carts so that Holmes would not spot them.

After a short distance, Holmes turned swiftly into a busy arcade of shops. Ozzie, Wiggins, and Pilar picked up their pace and followed, but soon they were jostled by the crowd and lost sight of him. They exited the arcade on the opposite end just in time to see Holmes accosted by two men. One man attempted to grab him, but he dodged the blow and threw the man to the ground.

As the other man raised a club, Ozzie and Wiggins dove at the back of his knees, which made him fall facedown on the cobblestones.

Meanwhile, the first man had gotten to his feet and charged at Holmes, who flipped him to the ground, where he stayed, dazed and groaning.

"Let us depart," Holmes said casually as he

herded Ozzie, Wiggins, and Pilar back into the busy arcade. "You simply disregarded my instructions and endangered yourselves in the process. I am trained to handle men like those. You are not."

Ozzie and Wiggins studied their moccasins and remained silent.

"But we were helping you," Pilar defended.

Holmes kept walking as though she had not spoken. Pilar fumed.

"I have a few details I must attend to before I depart, and I do not need to worry about the three of you following me around all of London. Now return to the carriage factory as I asked and prepare yourselves and the rest of the Irregulars to leave the city tomorrow. I will summon you later."

Holmes paused on the walkway, presumably to scold them more. Wiggins groaned inwardly.

Before Holmes could continue his lecture, a large piece of granite shattered just a few feet in front of them. They jumped off the walkway and followed Master's gaze to the roof of the building. They did not see anyone.

Holmes looked gravely into their solemn faces. "Need I say more?"

The three shook their heads.

"I will take a hansom to Scotland Yard, so you need not worry. Join the other Irregulars and keep together until you hear from me," he repeated as he waved down a cab. He climbed aboard and sped off, leaving Ozzie, Wiggins, and Pilar to race back to the Castle.

CHAPTER SIX

FAREWELL TO THE CASTLE

Wiggins smelled the smoke before he saw it. When he discovered the source, he tore down the street toward the gang, who had assembled in a pitiful menagerie on the walkway across from the Castle. He didn't know what to look at first, their cheerless faces or his home, reduced to ash.

Wiggins searched Rohan's and Elliot's faces, sooty and streaked with tears. The two just shook their heads, and Wiggins could not bring himself to ask for the details, for fear he would break down, too.

Instead, he followed Ozzie and Pilar to the archway, which had once framed the regal front doors, and peered inside. The roof had caved in completely to let in the sky. Burnt beams and shingles littered the floor. The interior walls were singed black. Tendrils of smoke curled up from the smoldering embers.

The fire company had arrived just in time to douse the fire and prevent it from spreading to the surrounding buildings. A few of the firemen had accused the Irregulars of setting flame to the place, but after seeing the looks on their faces, the men let it go.

Watching the shock register on Wiggins's face, Elliot could feel his mate's grief over the end of the only home he had ever known. Elliot recalled once again his own family's cottage in Dingle, claimed by a heartless blaze as well. He never thought he'd feel at home again, until Wiggins had discovered the Castle. Though the two boys had had their differences over the years, none of that mattered now.

Elliot walked over to Wiggins, slung an arm over his shoulder, and stood there quietly with him for a moment before explaining what had happened.

"There will be no rebuildin' it." Wiggins finally allowed himself to speak.

Elliot nodded, and both boys stood in silence. The Castle smelled badly at times. It could be damp and cold, even in the warmer months. The dirt portion of the floor was often muddy, and the roof leaked. But still, it was their own, their sanctuary from the streets, the police, and the workhouse. After the events of the morning, Wiggins couldn't help but wonder if all of this was a sign. He wasn't sure of what, but in a matter of hours, his whole world — his home, his work for Holmes, and his boys — seemed to be collapsing. He swallowed a lump in his throat and looked back at the gang sitting on the walkway, lost and bewildered. As best he could, he set aside his own fears and went to them.

"Well, boys, for me, and for some of you, the Castle was the only home we ever knew. And now, by some stroke of terrible luck, it's gone. But maybe it's true that when one door closes, another opens. Just this mornin', Ozzie, Pilar, and I met with Master, and he has offered us a paid adventure out of the city." Wiggins could tell that some of the boys were still dazed and he didn't have their full attention yet.

He motioned to Ozzie, who pulled the pound notes from his pocket and held them up for the gang. Their eyes grew large at the sum.

"It's true," Wiggins continued. "Master has provided enough *groat* to spend a few weeks some-where special, so special, in fact, he won't tell us about it until later today. We leave tomorrow."

At this, Alfie perked up. "Can we be highway-men and stop people on the road and take their money?"

Wiggins laughed. "I think we'll try to stay on the right side of the law, Elf."

Fletcher looked at the burned carriage factory. "It'll be nice to go somewheres."

"Maybe Master is sendin' us to Brighton Beach," said Simpson.

"I can't swim," said Pete.

"It's too cold anyway," said James.

As the boys traded guesses on their destination,

Ozzie crossed the street back to the Castle and stared at the remains.

Pilar tagged along. "Where will you all stay tonight? The eleven of you can't sleep on the street together. The police will arrest you. Maybe Mamá and I can make room for you in our flat."

Ozzie shrugged. "We'll figure it out, I suppose." His mind was elsewhere, and Pilar could sense it as she followed him to the trapdoor.

How could it be that the door was burned to a crisp but still standing? Ozzie wondered. And the stone wall that framed it remained intact. He studied a metal bar that was wedged diagonally between the trapdoor and the ground. He kicked the bar and dislodged it. The trapdoor fell into the building.

"What do you make of that?" Pilar asked.

"Master has set a trap for Moriarty's organization . . ." Ozzie mused aloud, but did not finish the thought. Smoke still hung in the air and made him cough.

"What do you mean?" Pilar studied him.

But Ozzie just reached into his coat for his tonic and swigged, then turned to cross the street.

Following, Pilar stewed. Ozzie could be so much like Master at times, disappearing into his own thoughts and neglecting to answer direct questions. The two of them could make her blood boil.

"Where we going to spend tonight?" Alfie was asking when Ozzie and Pilar rejoined the gang on the walkway.

"I know a few places," said Wiggins confidently. He looked at Ozzie, whose face was twisted in thought, or perhaps concern. "What is it, Oz?"

"Did you notice the metal bar wedged across the trapdoor? The fire was set on purpose. None of you — us — were supposed to survive."

A chorus of "Who did it?" and "Was it the Gents?" and "We'll get 'em!" broke out among the gang.

Ozzie said quietly, "I think it was Moriarty's men."

The boys froze. The mere mention of Moriarty scared them more than any fire.

Wiggins looked grave and asked Ozzie with his eyes if he was sure.

Ozzie nodded.

Wiggins motioned to the gang. "To Baker Street."

He took one last look at the Castle, then turned and did not look back.

CHAPTER SEVEN

THE BEARDED MAN
APPEARS

The Irregulars waited across from Holmes's flat for over an hour. Wiggins stroked Shirley's soft head.

"Master might not return until late," he said to Ozzie. "Maybe a few of us should go over to Dr. Watson's flat and see if he is there."

Pedestrians passed them on the walkway. Most were absorbed in conversation or walked too purposefully to notice them. But a few strollers tossed disapproving glances at the gang.

"What are you starin' at? Ain't you ever seen a handsome bloke before?" Alfie barked.

Wiggins put a hand on his shoulder and reminded him to keep his wits about him.

Just then, a slow-moving brougham approached. It was a curious-looking vehicle. The door had no windows, only a closed wood hatch at the top.

"That's a strange one," Rohan noted.

Elliot agreed. "Someone wants a bit of privacy."

"No. He's looking for somebody." Pilar turned to Ozzie and then to Wiggins.

They both nodded and stood.

Without a word, Ozzie crossed the street and squatted a few doors down from 221B. Though the brougham had not reached him yet, he could see the small hatch on the door slide open. The passenger compartment was dark, and Ozzie could not see anyone inside.

Gradually, the brougham made its way toward him. The tip of a spyglass peered out of the hatch. It was aimed directly at the window of Master's flat.

Whoever is in there, thought Ozzie, is not afraid of being noticed.

The brougham continued its measured pace. Cautiously, Ozzie followed on foot.

"Everyone, wait here and keep out of trouble," Wiggins told the gang as he tucked Shirley inside his coat. "Oz and I have a bit of investigatin' to do."

"I am coming with you," Pilar said matter-of-factly.

Alfie jumped up. "Me, too!"

"No, Elf. You, Rohan, and Elliot go to Dr. Watson's and see if Master is there. Report back here directly. We won't be long. The rest of you, remember, no trouble. Barnaby, you're in charge."

Everyone did as they were told, and Wiggins and Pilar ran off to catch Ozzie.

The brougham had picked up speed, and Ozzie was wheezing by the time they reached him. Wiggins put a hand on his shoulder as he jogged beside him. "Take it easy, mate. Do you have your tonic?"

Ozzie ignored him and kept on.

Wiggins searched the streets until he discovered a large hackney headed in the same direction as the brougham. The three climbed on its back.

After a short ride, the brougham pulled to the

side and a man with a cane exited. Ozzie, Pilar, and Wiggins hopped off the hackney and leaned casually against a wall so they could observe him.

The man was tall and wore a gray suit with a traditional cut and a gray silk top hat with a black band. His eyes were hidden by smoked lenses, and his mouth was concealed by the thickest beard they had ever seen, so thick in fact, that the man appeared more gorilla-like than human. Extending his walking stick forward, he approached.

Ozzie, Wiggins, and Pilar looked casually in various directions, doing their best to seem unaware, or at the very least, disinterested. They all held their breath as the bearded man passed. As soon as he turned the next corner, they trailed him.

"That's some beard," Wiggins said.

"And those glasses," Ozzie said. "They're what a blind man wears."

The three followed at a distance, and within minutes, Ozzie knew where the bearded man was going.

45

He turned onto the next street and stationed himself at a light pole a few doors down from Dr. Watson's residence.

Pilar looked at Ozzie and Wiggins. "What do we do now?"

"We wait," said Ozzie, motioning for them to crouch beside a stoop with him. "And pray that Rohan, Elliot, and Alfie know enough to be inconspicuous when they arrive."

CHAPTER EIGHT

A MEETING WITH DR. WATSON

houldn't we warn Dr. Watson?" asked Pilar after ten minutes had passed.

Ozzie shook his head. "The bearded man is waiting for Master. If we alert Watson, he will confront him, and that would be dangerous. We must wait. If Master appears, we can alert him."

Pilar looked at Ozzie with admiration. "You figure things out pretty quickly."

"I may be wrong. He could be waiting to burn down Dr. Watson's house like Moriarty's henchmen burned down the carriage factory." Ozzie shrugged. "But I think we should wait."

Wiggins had rarely heard Ozzie second-guess himself, and it made him uneasy. He pulled Shirley from inside his coat and stroked her.

Just then, Rohan, Elliot, and Alfie came around the corner at the opposite end of the street.

Wiggins held his breath, praying they did not notice or call attention to them.

Whether by luck or good judgment, the three boys continued down the street to Dr. Watson's residence and knocked on the door. The maid answered, kept them waiting a moment, and then showed them in.

Meanwhile, the bearded man kept his casual post.

Some time later, after filling in Dr. Watson on the events of the morning, Rohan, Elliot, and Alfie emerged from his flat. Watson had not seen Master and seemed very concerned. The boys assured him they would send word as soon as they found him.

As they started down the walkway, Alfie motioned with his chin to the bearded man. "Look at 'im. He's a scary one."

"I think he's watchin' us. Or maybe the doctor's place. Let's 'ave a look at 'im." Elliot headed down the street toward him.

"Elliot, wait —" Rohan tried to slow his friend down, but Elliot was stirred up.

"Say, guv, you waitin' for somebody?"

The man acted as though he had not heard.

Elliot's cheeks reddened. He balled his fingers into fists. Rohan reached out to put a hand on Elliot's shoulder. But Elliot pushed it off and stomped straight up to the bearded man.

"You, the one holdin' up the lamp pole, I *asked* if you was waitin' on somebody."

From a distance, Wiggins took in the whole scene, and groaned. When someone got under Elliot's skin, there was no stopping him. It was a good thing Rohan was there, both for his good sense and his strength. Still, even he might not stand a chance against the bearded man, who appeared taller than Master.

Elliot now stood just a few feet away from him. When he still didn't respond, Elliot pressed. "Well, *are* you?"

Finally provoked, the bearded man twisted the knob off his cane and pulled out a long narrow sword from its shaft. He grinned, revealing a set of large yellow teeth, and slashed the air around Elliot.

Ozzie, Wiggins, and Pilar let out a collective gasp and instinctively leapt around the corner to help.

Meanwhile, Rohan grabbed Elliot by the collar and pulled him back just as the sword blade sliced the air where his face had been.

The bearded man took two long strides toward them and thrust the sword out again, but tripped and fell onto the stone walkway. He lost his sword in the street.

Alfie ran to pick it up. Though it was bigger than he was, he swung it like a knight, yelling, "Aha, aha, aha!"

The bearded man pushed his way to his feet and chased Alfie. Fortunately, his long, clumsy strides seemed like they'd be no match for Alfie, who was quick as a jackrabbit.

Wiggins shook his head as he approached Elliot. "I know you are still outta sorts from this mornin', mate, but what were you thinkin', goin' after a thug like that? You gotta learn to control your temper, Stitch, or you're gonna get yourself and the rest of us hurt. Now go make sure that bloke doesn't nab Alfie."

Elliot's face was red from anger or maybe embarrassment. For once, he didn't argue or give Wiggins any lip. He just dutifully ran off. Rohan nodded to Wiggins and followed.

Pilar stood watching the boys with her arms crossed. "That bearded man seems quite the oaf."

Before the boys could answer, they saw Master standing only a few feet away. How long had he been there? Had he witnessed the row? Ozzie shrunk at the thought of Master's condemnation.

Wiggins didn't think he could stomach another scolding.

But if Master had seen or disapproved, he kept it to himself. Matter-of-factly, he said, "How convenient that you are here. Let us visit Watson together, shall we?"

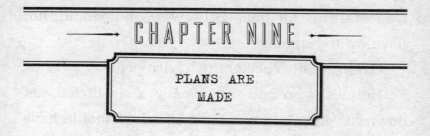

CHAPTER NINE

PLANS ARE
MADE

ne of Moriarty's men was outside my residence!" Watson appeared more outraged than
afraid.

They sat in Watson's study, drinking tea and
eating biscuits that the maid had served. After
Wiggins had updated Holmes and Watson on the
burning of the carriage factory and the encounter
with the bearded man, he devoured two biscuits
and struggled to gracefully sip his tea and hold the
saucer at the same time. Would he ever grow accustomed to proper etiquette? How was it that Pilar
made it seem so effortless and always looked like a
proper young lady with the social graces of a much
wealthier and more educated girl?

"I believe Osgood is quite right, Watson. The man conducting surveillance outside your home was waiting for me. Otherwise, he would not have waited so long."

Ozzie felt his cheeks flush with pride.

Holmes, who had taken nary a sip of tea, set down his cup and saucer and stood. "I should have anticipated that Moriarty would send his men after the Irregulars so soon."

"What about the man we followed here?" Pilar asked. "Do you know who he is?"

Holmes shook his head and paced the study. "I am familiar with many people in Moriarty's organization, but the man you have described is distinctive in appearance. He may have been engaged especially for the occasion."

"Well, he's gone now and the boys have nowhere to stay. How are you going to help them?" Pilar met Holmes's gaze straight on.

He waved away her concern. "Fear not, Señorita, arrangements have been made. Wiggins and Osgood, you and the rest of the Irregulars will be the guests of Mr. John Bloomfield at his farm outside of Haywards Heath."

"Bloomfield," said Watson. "Didn't he assist you in the case of the Garden Court Swindler?"

"The very same," Holmes confirmed. "Bloomfield and his son will arrive with their cart tomorrow morning and drive you out to their farm. You will be their guests for two weeks. By the time you return to London, we will have located new accommodations for you." Holmes nodded to Pilar, who smiled in return.

"Will you be leaving London as well?" Ozzie asked.

"In the morning, Watson and I will depart for the Continent. I have planned a short trip. We shall return in one week's time."

As Master spoke, Ozzie couldn't help but wonder, Was he holding something back? Why was he leaving for the Continent? Ozzie's mind clicked with speculation, but the feeling that most overwhelmed him was jealousy. Watson would be traveling alone with Holmes for an entire week while Ozzie was being carted off to the countryside.

Holmes turned back to Pilar. "As for you, Señorita, I do not anticipate any danger for you or Madam Estrella. Your involvement with our investigations has never given away your usual whereabouts."

"Where will the boys sleep tonight?" Pilar asked.

"I have considered that." Holmes smiled at Watson.

"All of them, here? My flat is hardly safe under the circumstances." But even as Watson protested, there was a tone of defeat in his voice. And he agreed, since his wife was away visiting relatives, that the Irregulars could spend the night. He and the maid would make room for them in the common areas of their home.

Glad to have that settled, Holmes proceeded to give Watson detailed instructions on how and where to meet him at Victoria Station the following morning.

Thoughts of Holmes's departure and his own preyed on Ozzie. Besides that morning, Ozzie had not seen Master for several weeks, and now he likely would not see him for at least a few more. All of the missed opportunities to speak with him flooded his brain, and now, more than ever, he regretted not trying. It was a simple question really: Are you my father? Frustrated, Ozzie ran his hands through his hair.

Pilar watched Ozzie staring intently at Master. She could tell that he had been talking to himself inside. What was he thinking? She had grown accustomed to Ozzie's moodiness, but it troubled her that she could not read him as she could most people. It was clear that something Master had said disturbed him. But what? Ever since Ozzie had returned from his trip to Oxfordshire, he seemed distracted whenever they were around Master. Why *was* that?

Holmes rubbed his hands together and then clasped them. "Watson, if you would be so good as to let me climb over the fence in the garden, just in case I am being followed by someone with a bit more subtlety than the bearded fellow our young friends saw earlier?"

"Holmes, you should stay," Watson implored.

"No, my friend. I am dangerous company right now. It would be best if we do not meet again until tomorrow."

With that, Holmes bowed to Wiggins, Ozzie, and Pilar, and disappeared.

CHAPTER TEN

GOOD-BYE
TO PILAR

don't think I'm the farmer type," Wiggins said. "I
don't care much for large animals. Still, farmers
eat hearty breakfasts, right? And I've never left
the city before. I might like that."

Wiggins and Ozzie were walking Pilar back to
her flat near Covent Garden Market. In spite of her
assurances that she would be fine on her own,
Wiggins had insisted. On the way, they had met up
with the rest of the gang on Baker Street and
instructed them to go to Watson's. Happily they
ran off, relieved to have a place for the night.

"Maybe you'll learn to milk a cow and ride a
horse."

Wiggins couldn't tell if it was mockery or

jealousy he detected in Pilar's voice. "I don't know about touchin' any cow, but climbin' onto a horse, now that would be grand — just like one of 'em American cowboys we were readin' about, right, Oz?"

It took Ozzie a few seconds to answer. "Why do you think Master is leaving for the Continent tomorrow?"

"Maybe he wants things with Moriarty to pass before he returns. There've been at least three attempts on Master's life today. You can't blame 'im for wantin' to go somewhere it's safe." Wiggins dodged a well-dressed man on the walkway as they continued to Pilar's flat.

"It's unlike Master to flee from trouble," Ozzie said as much to himself as to the others.

"Maybe he's protecting Dr. Watson," Pilar offered, "by making sure he leaves London."

"That's true," Wiggins agreed. "It may be dangerous for Watson to stay, and you know he wouldn't leave town without Master. He would stay here and try to help him." Wiggins sighed when he saw a muffin man pushing an empty cart home for the night. The biscuits he'd eaten at Watson's had long been digested, and he had not had supper. He hoped Watson's maid would feed them when they returned.

"Maybe," Ozzie said, unconvinced. "But I think there is more. Master has set an elaborate trap to catch Moriarty and his organization, and then he decides to leave London just days before they are all to be arrested? It doesn't make sense. Why would he leave it to Scotland Yard to make all the arrests? He always complains about their sloppy work." Ozzie shook his head. "There is something else, something we are missing."

Wiggins had to agree. "It does sound unlike Master to run off, especially when the job is not done. He likes the action too much. Did you notice how energetic he was today? I think the attempts on his life excite him."

"What is it then? Is there something more on the Continent? Is that why he's going?" Pilar turned onto a narrow street, and the boys followed.

"It's about —" Ozzie stopped and leaned against a brick building.

"You all right, Oz?" Wiggins stopped, too, and looked at his friend curiously.

"Moriarty!"

"What about him?" Pilar and Wiggins said at the same time.

"Master is leaving for the Continent knowing that Moriarty will follow. If Master remains in London, Moriarty may be arrested, but he will most likely get away like he has before, like he always does. . . ."

Ozzie tapped his right temple with his index finger. "But, if Master leaves London, Moriarty will not hesitate to follow. He will avoid capture and can also hunt down Master."

Wiggins looked at Ozzie in awe. "You mean Master is actin' like bait?"

"Exactly," Ozzie confirmed.

Pilar was equally amazed by Ozzie's deduction skills. The pieces began to line up in her mind, too. "If Master plans to apprehend Moriarty himself, he will need our help."

Ozzie nodded.

"What are you sayin'? That we go to the

Continent to protect Master from *the most danger-ous man in all of England*?" Wiggins pulled his hair. "That's mad!"

But Ozzie would not be deterred. "We will fol-low Master and wait to see if Moriarty appears. If he does, we will follow him." Ozzie could feel his pulse pound with excitement.

"I don't think Master will care for this plan, Oz. How many times has he warned us 'bout puttin' ourselves in harm's way? I see the logic in it, but how will we be able to warn Master before trouble happens, especially when dealin' with Moriarty?"

Ozzie clapped Wiggins on the shoulder. "We will figure out a way, mate."

Wiggins and Pilar frowned, each for their own reasons.

"And what will I do while you two travel abroad? Sit here? You've never even left England. You only speak English! I have traveled in eight other countries. You need me."

Ozzie looked at Pilar thoughtfully. "We never suggested that you couldn't come. But what would your mum say?"

Pilar stamped her foot. "*Que mala suerte*. Such bad luck. You two can go on all the adventures you want while I'm stuck at home with Mamá, attending dreary lessons."

Wiggins, who right now would not have minded trading places with Pilar, mumbled, "At least you have a home . . . and a mother."

The three walked in heavy silence.

When they reached Pilar's building, Ozzie said, "Why don't you ask her if you can join us?"

"She will never say yes. And if I go without her permission, she will worry herself sick. I am stuck." Pilar bit her lip to prevent tears.

Then she impulsively hugged both boys. "Take care of each other, and come back as quickly as you can."

Before either of them could say anything in return, she ran up the stairs to her flat without looking back.

CHAPTER ELEVEN

THE END OF SOMETHING

Early the next morning, while waiting on the steps outside Watson's flat, Ozzie and Wiggins said their good-byes and told the gang they would meet up with them again in about two weeks' time.

No one had slept much the night before. They were all too wound up from the events of yesterday and anxious about their travels to the countryside. Wiggins pulled Rohan and Elliot aside. "Now remember, I need you two to take charge. The boys aren't used to farm life. Keep 'em workin' and listen to what Farmer Bloomfield says, and the time will pass quickly."

Elliot nodded. He understood the plan, and

though he and Rohan had already expressed concern over Ozzie and Wiggins's safety, he assured Wiggins that they'd keep things under control. "We can handle the boys a few weeks, but what are we gonna do with no place to stay when our time in the countryside is done?"

"We'll work it out, Stitch. Oz and I will be back in London before the rest of you. We'll find somethin'. And Master said he would help."

Alfie had been hovering nearby. "I still don't understand why I can't go with the two of you. Farms are dull. I want adventure."

"Enough *rabbit*. When have you ever been on a farm, Elf? It could be heaps of fun. Besides, if too many of us go, Master will discover us."

"And the other boys will need your help," Ozzie added.

Alfie smiled at the thought. "How?"

Ozzie looked at Wiggins for an answer.

"Because I am good with animals?" Alfie suggested.

"Right," said Wiggins, remembering Alfie's affection for a stray dog he'd once dragged in.

"And I need you to care for Shirley. Our travels would be too much for her." Wiggins pulled the ferret from inside his coat, kissed her head, and handed her to Alfie.

Gently taking the animal, Alfie grinned and puffed up his chest with pride. "You can bet I will, boss."

John Bloomfield and his son Jerry soon arrived with a large farm cart pulled by two tall horses. Bloomfield was a broad man with thick arms and large, rugged hands. His red beard was sprinkled with gray, and his sky blue eyes had a smile about them. Jerry was just about fully grown and was a slimmer, clean-shaven version of his father.

At Wiggins's prompting, the Irregulars introduced themselves one at a time and shook Bloomfield's and Jerry's hands as they boarded the cart.

Bloomfield laughed good-naturedly at the boys' formality. "Well, Jerry, I guess we have a crew of city gentlemen here."

Elliot was the last of the boys to board the cart. After giving a knowing nod to Wiggins and Ozzie, he bowed his head shyly and shook Bloomfield's hand. He did the same with Jerry. Watching Elliot, Wiggins realized there was more to the surly bloke after all.

The Bloomfields climbed into the front of the cart, and the elder man said, "Mr. Holmes's wire instructed me to pick up the lot of you."

"Don't worry about us," said Ozzie. "We have some friends who are expecting us to visit."

Bloomfield's expression told Ozzie that he didn't believe him. But he just nodded and gently slapped the reins. The horses lurched forward, then pulled the cart with a steady gait.

As Wiggins watched the gang ride away, part of him felt relieved not having to worry over their safety for the next few weeks. Yet their separation felt like the end of something. . . .

Wiggins looked at Ozzie, whose eyes seemed to gleam in the first light of day. He thought about the possibility of meeting up with Moriarty on the Continent. In some ways, Ozzie was just like Master, relishing the danger that awaited them. Wiggins wished he could be more like that. But it just wasn't in his nature.

When the cart was halfway down the road, Alfie stood up and waved. Wiggins nodded and waved back.

It was just him and Oz now. He tried to feel excited about the private time with his best mate. But as the cart continued down the street and disappeared, a troubled feeling worked its way into his gut. Maybe he just needed a good breakfast.

CHAPTER TWELVE

A SURPRISE VISITOR

An hour or so later, Ozzie and Wiggins watched from a distance as Dr. Watson let the first and second hansom cabs pass before hailing the third. The boys were ready and quickly stole a ride on the back of a mail coach headed in the same direction. They remembered Master's instructions to Watson the day before — to assist in evading anyone who might be trailing him. Watson followed the instructions precisely.

After traveling down a few streets in the relative quiet of early morning, Watson hopped out of his hansom and dashed through the same arcade the boys had been in the day before. He exited the other side and climbed into a waiting brougham.

With no time to find another carriage, Ozzie and Wiggins climbed onto the back of Watson's.

As they did so, Ozzie caught a glimpse of the driver — a rotund man with a scarf tied about his neck and the lower portion of his face. If he noticed them, he said nothing.

They rode in a roundabout fashion to Victoria Station, where Watson exited the brougham and strode swiftly inside.

When Ozzie and Wiggins slipped off the back, the driver said, "Keep your distance, boys, or he will see you and send you back."

His words stopped them in their tracks. The man heaved his substantial bulk off the driver's seat and down onto the street, where he faced them. Neither of the boys recognized him.

He handed Wiggins a card along with a ten-pound note. "If you meet with any trouble, send me a wire. Sherlock says you can conduct surveillance better than anyone. Following him and the professor unobserved will be your ultimate test.

"Remember, track the hunters, not the prey. Sherlock's plans are brilliant, but even he cannot anticipate everything. If you really wish to help my brother, watch and report, but do not interfere."

So this was Master's older brother?! The boys had heard of him, but had never met him.

Ozzie looked at the card in Wiggins's hand.

"My-croft Holmes," Wiggins read out loud. "Di-og, Di-og —"

"Diogenes Club," Ozzie read over his shoulder.

"You should be off before you miss the train," Mycroft said. "Remember, follow Moriarty — observe and keep a safe distance. You can wire me at the Diogenes Club if you need assistance." With that, he climbed back up into the driver's seat and slapped the reins. The horse's hooves clacked against the cobblestones, and in a moment, Mycroft was gone.

Inside Victoria Station, the boys did not see Watson anywhere. But they knew he would be meeting Holmes on the Continental Express. After asking a porter its whereabouts, the boys bought two third-class tickets and raced to find their track.

The black and green engine had already begun to puff smoke. Steam hissed from its sides like some mechanical dragon. The boys approached the train with its low-hung sliding windows and wood carriages painted green. As they passed the car second from the front, they spied Dr. Watson sitting on a velvet upholstered seat in a first-class compartment. Across from him sat a priest wearing a large round-rimmed hat.

"Where's Master?" Wiggins asked, concerned. "The two are supposed to be together."

Ozzie laughed. "He's right there, across from Dr. Watson."

Wiggins looked again. "You mean the priest?"

"After all these years of working for Master, his disguises still fool you, mate. It looks like he is fooling Watson, too." Ozzie grinned as the train whistle blew.

The boys ran to the rear of the train and boarded the open-air, third-class carriage. It had a roof overhead and a railing around the perimeter to keep passengers from falling off.

As the train began to chug forward, something

73

on the far side of the station caught Ozzie's eye. He paused on the steps. Professor Moriarty, in a top hat and black cape, had entered with another man. Ozzie thought it was Colonel Moran. They were too late to make the train, but Ozzie was sure they would find a way to follow. With a mix of nervousness and excitement, he stepped into the carriage.

He made his way over to Wiggins, who stood in the rear talking to another passenger. Wasn't it just like his best mate to make friends as soon as they had boarded the train? He shook his head. He dreaded making idle chatter with strangers, particularly when there were so many more important things to consider.

As Ozzie approached, the person turned and flashed him a spirited smile. "You didn't think I would let you roam about alone on the Continent, did you?"

"But how —"

Pilar raised an eyebrow. "I have my ways. I'm a Baker Street Irregular, remember?" She smacked the railing, tossed her hair back against the breeze, and laughed. "Now then, we're not exactly traveling first class, are we? But I suppose this will do. *¡Vámanos!*" she exclaimed as the train pulled away from the station. "Let's go!"

— CHAPTER THIRTEEN —

A TRIP TO THE COUNTRYSIDE

So where do you think Oz and Wiggins are now?" Alfie asked Rohan.

"Elf, I'm gonna smash your *loaf*," Elliot growled. "You been askin' the same question every five minutes since we left 'em."

Rohan patted Alfie's shoulder. "They are likely on the train now, mate. They'll be all right."

Alfie nodded as he gazed down the dirt road. From his perch in the back of Bloomfield's cart, London looked like a large gray smudge on the horizon. The traffic of the city was behind them, and the carriage wheels bumped along the dirt road southward to Haywards Heath. On either side of the road, green grass and meadows stretched out as far as the eye could see, interrupted now and again by small buildings in nearby villages and towns.

Though clouds hung in the April sky, everything appeared lighter and brighter. The crisp emerald color of the grass stood in stark contrast to the brown dirt road. The air was different, too. Instead of fog and sewer smells, it carried a sweetness, and Alfie found himself opening his mouth to taste it.

Hardly a word passed between the boys during the ride. Instead, they lounged quietly and watched the scenery. They listened to birds chirping and the rhythmic sound of the horses' hooves and the rolling cart wheels.

"It sure is quiet," Rohan observed.

"Yeah," Shem agreed.

"I don't know if I like it," Pete said warily.

"This is paradise," Elliot assured him.

"Everything feels, feels . . ." Alfie tried to find the right words to describe the countryside.

"Peaceful," finished James.

Bloomfield laughed. "Boys, this is still too busy

for us. There are towns surrounding us. Wait till we drive a little farther, then you'll see the heart of the south country!" Bloomfield began to hum and then sang,

> *"In prime of years, when I was young,*
> *I took delight in youthful toys,*
> *Not knowing then what did belong*
> *Unto the pleasure of those days.*
> *At seven years old I was child,*
> *And subject to be beguiled."*

"I'm seven, I think," Alfie said. "Or maybe eight now."

Bloomfield smiled and kept singing.

The boys listened contentedly to the song's story about growing up and growing old. But what they liked even more than the words was Bloomfield's voice, which reminded them of Wiggins's. And though none would admit it, the sound comforted them.

* * *

A little before midday, they stopped at a roadside stream to water the horses. A grove of beech trees clustered on the opposite side of the road, and pastures sprawled in the distance. The boys clambered out of the cart.

Jerry heaved a burlap sack from under the driver's seat and joined them. He pulled out a large loaf of bread and a round of cheese, which he cut with a knife. Then he handed out slices of each. They sat in a circle around him and ate without speaking.

After all the boys had been fed, Jerry fixed himself a snack. "Working for Mr. Sherlock Holmes must be exciting," he said.

"We've had some granventures," said Alfie with a mouth full of food.

"He means grand adventures," said Elliot.

"It can be exciting," said Rohan. "But sometimes we just sit around and wait for work. That's the hard part."

Jerry smiled. "You'll like it on the farm then. There's always a lot of work, from the time you wake up until the time you eat dinner. But I don't know how exciting you'll find it."

"What will we be doing?" asked Elliot.

"We work a cattle farm, so you will be helping to take care of cows mostly. Feeding them, cleaning out the barn, moving them to different pastures, fixing fences, and the like. We've plenty of work for you."

"Can I learn how to ride a horse?" asked Alfie.

"Maybe," said Jerry. "I had my own horse by the time I was your age, so I can't see why you shouldn't give it a try."

Alfie jumped up, stuck the remaining piece of bread and cheese in his pocket, walked over to the horses that had been pulling their cart, and patted one of them on the side. "I have a way with animals," he told Jerry.

The horse shook its head and let out a loud whinny, which caused Alfie to jump back and land on his bottom.

The boys all laughed.

"I can see that," said Jerry with a smile. "I think you'll do just fine on the farm."

CHAPTER FOURTEEN

RIDING THE CONTINENTAL EXPRESS

Smoke from the engine blew through the third-class carriage of the Continental Express. Ozzie coughed and Wiggins rubbed his eyes. But Pilar beamed as she held fast to the railing while the train chugged and lurched. She closed her eyes and turned her face to the dim, mid-morning sun.

Still coughing, Ozzie managed to take a swig of his tonic. He held up the small amber bottle and wondered if he had enough for the trip.

"Tell us," Wiggins pressed Pilar, "how did you escape your mum?"

"I knew Mamá would never let me go, so I told a small lie."

Ozzie stared out the back of the train, half

listening. The other part of his mind was occupied with the adventure that lay ahead.

"I said I wanted to visit my uncle in Liverpool. Mamá knew I was up to something, but we had been talking about a visit for a long time. We will be back in London by the time she realizes I am not with him, I hope."

"But she'll blame us when she finds out." Wiggins shook his head.

"Quit worrying, Wiggins. Mamá always knows that I am responsible. Now what is our plan for helping Master?"

Wiggins told her about Mycroft and his advice. Then he gazed out the back of the train with Ozzie.

By now, they had left London and were passing towns to the southeast of the city. All around them were rolling hills, dotted with trees and early spring flowers. Wiggins thought it looked pretty, but at the same time, too open and too bright. He'd take fog and streets thick with people over any country road.

"Are you okay?" Pilar asked him.

"Just thinkin' about London. I've never left before."

Pilar patted his shoulder. "You'll be fine."

Wiggins nodded. Then they both turned to Ozzie, who looked as though he was in a trance.

I hope he's not goin' to be in his 'ead the whole trip, thought Wiggins.

I wish I knew what was preying on him, Pilar said to herself.

"The train line ends in Dover, which is about three hours away," Wiggins said, attempting to gain Ozzie's attention. "Then, we catch a steamer across to —"

"Calais, France," Pilar finished.

When Wiggins gave her a questioning look, she said smartly, "I know the route, Wiggins. I traveled it a few times when Mamá and I were with the Grand Barboza Circus."

Wiggins nodded, recalling now that Pilar had traveled throughout much of Europe. Perhaps she would be more useful to have on this trip than he had realized.

Meanwhile, Ozzie considered how Master's plan

was unfolding. Moriarty and Moran were already chasing him, but how would they get to the steamer? A horse and carriage would not be fast enough. They would have to hire a private train. Ozzie craned his neck over the railing and looked down the tracks. He did not see any other trains. It is only a matter of time, he thought. Master was too clever to get caught at the port. He would make it to the Continent, but what then?

"We are out of order," he said.

"What?" Pilar and Wiggins waited for him to finish the thought.

"We are following Master and Watson when we should be following Moriarty and Moran."

"Moriarty and Moran?" Wiggins said.

"They were at the train station as we pulled out."

"That's perfect!" said Wiggins. "We have barely begun the trip, and they are already on Master's trail."

Pilar pinched her eyebrows together and was about to inquire further when Ozzie explained. "Mycroft was right. We can only really help Master if we trail the men who are trailing him. Master is not fleeing but luring. He wants Moriarty to follow, but he doesn't want to be caught. Not yet."

"So how can we help?" Wiggins asked.

"Like we always do, by observing and reporting."

Pilar nodded. "We can track Moriarty and make sure he doesn't trap Master."

Wiggins looked at Ozzie. "What do you think Moriarty and Moran are doing now?"

"My guess is that they are hiring a special — a private train, an engine with only one or two carriages — that can chase us without having to stop."

"Can they do that?" Wiggins said, wondering how on earth anyone could arrange such a thing.

"I believe so," said Ozzie.

"I thought only Queen Victoria had a private train," Pilar said in awe.

CHAPTER FIFTEEN

OZZIE DEDUCES
MASTER'S PLAN

At the Canterbury East Station, Ozzie, Wiggins, and Pilar watched the third-class carriage empty. No new passengers boarded.

Outside, the low-lying gray clouds had lifted and turned to puffy white, floating in a bowl of pale blue sky.

Pilar stretched in the open space and loosened her cape. "It looks like we'll have a nice trip to Dover. I'd forgotten how clear the air can be outside of London. It's a shame we can't see the cathedral from here. It's quite grand."

Wiggins stood and leaned over the railing so that the sun shined on his pale face. He motioned for Ozzie to join them. "C'mon, mate. If Moriarty's train comes speedin' up from behind, you'll see it soon enough."

In truth, Ozzie had, for the moment, put aside thoughts of Moriarty and was dwelling on Master. Would he have another opportunity to speak with him alone? He couldn't help but continue to chastise himself for not having approached him already. Even if he's not my father, he thought, why not ask and get it over with?

Wiggins nudged him with his foot, and he stood.

"Sorry, Wiggins, I guess I haven't been much of a traveling partner. It's a good thing Pilar is here."

Wiggins gave him a gentle shove. "There's still time to improve yourself, mate."

Ozzie laughed good-naturedly.

The conductor had entered their carriage and gave them a disapproving glance. The train began its chug forward.

Sensing a rare moment when Ozzie was fully present, Pilar said, "I've been wanting to ask you something, Ozzie, and I hope you won't get upset with me." She paused and took a breath. "Since you've come back from your travels in Oxfordshire, you have been different. You disappear into your thoughts more often. And frankly, sometimes it feels as though you are keeping a secret from us."

Wiggins's eyes widened.

Ozzie looked from Pilar to Wiggins. Why not tell them? he thought. They are my best friends. But as he practiced the words inside his head, it all sounded so ridiculous. What were the chances that Sherlock Holmes was actually his father? He looked at Pilar and Wiggins, their eyes intent, waiting for his reply. Even if it is ridiculous, I can tell them, he coaxed himself. He opened his mouth to speak, and then, over Pilar's shoulder, he saw them.

Without a word, Ozzie pointed to the platform where two men stood beside a luggage cart.

"Master!" Wiggins exclaimed. "And Watson."

"Why have they left the train?" Pilar's voice was strained. "Shall we jump?"

"There will be *no* jumping off this train." The conductor sneered humorlessly at the three of them before entering the second-class carriage.

As the train moved farther from the station,

they watched Master and Watson grow smaller. Wiggins groaned. "What are we supposed to do now?"

"Even if the train stops, we'll never be able to catch them," Pilar said.

Ozzie smiled and shook his head. "You see that?"

They followed his finger to where it pointed down the tracks. At first, they didn't see anything. Then black smoke appeared. From a distance, they made out what looked like a small engine with one or two coaches attached.

"You think that's the 'special'?" Pilar asked. "Hired by Moriarty?"

Ozzie nodded. "He doesn't know Master and Watson left the train. He'll follow our train to Dover, maybe follow us all the way to France."

"But how does that help us?" Wiggins asked.

"When Moriarty catches up with us, we will be able to follow him, just as Mycroft advised."

Wiggins looked concerned. "What if he *doesn't* find Master? What if he just finds *us*?"

CHAPTER SIXTEEN

FARM LIFE

Haywards Heath was lined with cobblestone streets and shops and houses of Tudor design. On the edge of the village, stone walls, fences, and gates marked the grounds of an empty cattle market. As Bloomfield drove the cart out of town, the road began to climb.

"Are you okay now, Alfie?" Rohan asked with a hint of laughter in his voice.

Alfie scowled at him. "I am tellin' you, Ro, I saw Gorilla-man in town. He was sittin' in a carriage — *waitin'*. Remember, he chased me yesterday, I got a *butcher's* at 'im."

"Elf, you were runnin' so fast, you didn't

even 'ave time to look over your shoulder." Elliot laughed.

"How would he know to come here?" Rohan reasoned. "No one was followin' us." He patted Alfie on the arm. "We'll be just fine, mate. Look around, we're in the beautiful, quiet countryside now — about to have an adventure."

Alfie nodded. But he knew who he saw, even if he didn't see him so well yesterday.

"There it is," said Jerry.

The Irregulars sat up and looked out across rolling green pastures, separated from the road by hedgerows. Down the hill stood a cluster of old stone buildings, some so covered with moss they appeared to be sprouting up from the earth. Among them, a stone farmhouse with a slate roof, an enormous barn, and a few other smaller buildings huddled together. Bloomfield turned the cart toward them. In the surrounding pastures and hills, large cows with shaggy reddish hair grazed.

"Welcome to Bloomfield's fields!" he boomed proudly.

The boys looked around. There were no people in sight. And it was so quiet. Only the occasional moo of the cows broke the silence.

"It's like we're all alone in the middle of nowhere," Rohan observed.

"I don't think I like it," said Pete.

Elliot's jaw hung open. "It's beautiful."

"Aw, ain't it so pretty," Alfie taunted.

For once, Elliot ignored Alfie.

"Look at all them cows," said Shem.

"Can we eat one?" asked Alfie.

Bloomfield laughed. "Hungry enough for a cow already? And I haven't even put you to work yet. Today you'll get settled. Jerry will show you around the place and lay out your chores. Tomorrow you work. And after you work, you may find some beef on your plate."

CHAPTER SEVENTEEN

A STRANGER
APPEARS

Mrs. Bloomfield was a round, no-nonsense woman who, after meeting the boys, gave them each a biscuit and some water and then told her husband to get to work; having guests didn't mean he was on holiday. "That goes for you, too, Jerry-berry," she said. Jerry blushed at the use of his nickname, and Bloomfield laughed and told the boys they could see who was the boss on the farm.

The boys watched the Bloomfields with rapt attention. In London, they saw parents and children walking together on the street or in the park, but they rarely witnessed such personal interaction. The Bloomfields were a family, which felt comforting somehow, even though it wasn't their family.

Obligingly, Jerry led them outside, across a dirt drive, and into a long rectangular building. Inside was a single large room with a row of hand-hewn wooden beds, each with a mattress, sheet, blanket, and pillow. A few small tables lined the perimeter. Sunlight from three six-paned windows flooded the space.

"We used to have a few farmhands that lived on the place, but no more. They all live in town now. So you boys have your own quarters."

Though simple and bare, the room was welcoming. The stone floor and walls appeared scrubbed clean. And few of the Irregulars had ever had a proper bed or bedding. Alfie ran his hand across the thin, soft pillow and woolly blanket.

"If you want to leave anything in here, go ahead, it's your place for the next few weeks." Jerry paused, realizing that the boys didn't have anything with them besides their clothes and whatever they carried in their pockets.

The boys just gazed about in awe.

Jerry clapped his hands. "All right then, let's go meet some of the ladies."

"I don't like girls," Alfie said as Jerry led them back outside and across the yard to the barn.

Jerry laughed. "Well, most of the girls are out grazing, but there are a few babes in here." Ten calves stood in wood stalls facing them.

"Oh, I get it," Alfie said. "Can I touch one? I'm good with animals." Gently, he stroked the nose of the smallest calf.

Before Jerry could say anything, the other boys began patting the calves as well.

"The ladies are pretty gentle creatures. Most of what you'll be doing is helpin' with them. Feeding, watering, moving them about, and makin' sure they don't run off. It sounds easy, but . . ." Jerry paused when something outside the barn door caught his eye. "Just a minute," he said as he stepped out.

The boys peered out as well. A dogcart had turned off the road onto the dirt path that led to the farm.

"You know them?" Elliot asked when Jerry returned.

Jerry shook his head.

Rohan looked from Elliot to Jerry and back again. "What if Alfie was right?"

The cart continued its approach. Detecting Rohan's concern, Jerry said, "I'll go get my dad. Meanwhile, just to be safe, all of you go up into the hayloft and hide behind the bales."

Jerry departed and the gang, led by Rohan, scurried to the ladder that led to the second level of the barn some twenty feet in the air. The hayloft ran half the width and the full length of the barn. Bales were stacked three or four high, like large building blocks. A few ropes with hooks and hoists were positioned throughout the barn.

Rohan made his way to a small set of doors that opened out the front of the barn. He peered through a crack. "If there is trouble, we can't let Jerry and Bloomfield deal with it alone."

Elliot, who had joined him at his perch, agreed.

In the yard below, the farmers stood together talking. Then Jerry proceeded to the house and Bloomfield resumed throwing feed to the chickens casually.

Rohan and Elliot watched the cart pull into the yard. Sitting inside was the bearded man.

Alfie crawled up behind them and peered through the crack in the doors as well. "I told ya I saw 'im!"

"Shhhh!" Elliot clapped a hand over Alfie's mouth and whispered to Rohan, "What now?"

Neither of them was often in the position to make such decisions. Suddenly, Ozzie and Wiggins's absence weighed on them.

"I think we should wait and see," Rohan suggested.

"But he knows we're here. If he works for Moriarty, he ain't gonna let Bloomfield stand in his way."

Rohan realized Elliot was right. He thought for a moment and then said, "Okay, I have an idea."

CHAPTER EIGHTEEN

A BRAWL
BREAKS OUT

ir, I saw you drive a cart full of dirty children through the village only a short time ago. I ask again, where are they?" The bearded man stood in the cart, his shadow looming menacingly over Bloomfield.

The driver of the cart, a burly man whose suit appeared a size too small for him, sat silently on his perch beside him.

Bloomfield continued to throw feed to the chickens. "I'll admit, sir, that I did drive children to my door, but I was met here by my friend Sherlock Holmes, who in his own carriage drove off with them to the south." Bloomfield pointed down the road away from the town.

"I will not be lied to by a bumpkin. The tracks of a carriage show in the path up to your house. No carriage tracks lead away."

Bloomfield placed the feed bucket on the ground, walked over to the carriage, and rolled up his sleeves. He wore the matter-of-fact expression of a man about to conduct some business.

The bearded man lifted his walking stick and twisted its knob in an agitated fashion.

Suddenly, loud clanging erupted, causing the horses to neigh and buck and the cart to lurch forward, which sent the bearded man tumbling to the ground.

Alfie stood directly in front of the horses with a large milk can in one hand and a ladle in the other. As he continued to bang, he shouted to Bloomfield, "I told ya I had a way with animals!"

Bloomfield laughed. "Yes, I see that, son!"

Meanwhile, the cart driver attempted to gain control of the horses as the bearded man stood up and lunged at Alfie. Bloomfield threw his large body between the two, only to be struck with the cane and hurled to the ground. The bearded man then extracted the sword from his cane and chased Alfie across the yard.

With the horses now settled, the cart driver followed.

Alfie led them into the barn and scrambled up the ladder leading to the hayloft. The bearded man pursued him and instructed his driver to remain on the ground. But the sword made it difficult for the bearded man to follow Alfie up the ladder. He stopped, reinserted the sword inside the cane, which he hooked over his shoulder, and then climbed awkwardly.

When he finally reached the top, Rohan leapt out from behind a pile of hay and pushed two bales off the loft. As they fell, a rope unfurled and a pulley spun wildly.

The snare caught the bearded man's right ankle, tightened, and yanked him upside down. He hit the roof of the barn with a thud.

Furious, he pulled his sword out again and slashed at the rope that held him. After a few tries, he sliced it, causing him to drop headfirst and strike the edge of the loft and then fall another twenty feet to the barn floor. He lay motionless.

His driver stood stunned. Before he could decide what to do, he was met at the door by Bloomfield, wielding a pitchfork, and Jerry, carrying a hunting rifle.

"Why don't you have a seat, sir, while the wife raises the constable?" Bloomfield grinned as the man lowered himself helplessly to a bale of hay.

Sensing it was now safe, the Irregulars popped up from their positions in various parts of the loft.

While they congratulated one another on a job well done, Jerry walked over to the bearded man and nudged him with the toe of his boot. He remained unconscious, his nose, mouth, and beard bloodied from the fall.

Bloomfield looked at the ragtag gang up in his hayloft and laughed. "Mr. Holmes said you boys knew how to take care of yourselves."

CHAPTER NINETEEN

DIGGING
FOR DISGUISE

There's no one comin', keep searchin'." Wiggins stood guard as Ozzie and Pilar rummaged through the suitcases in the baggage compartment.

"Here's something for me." Pilar held up a fitted gray dress with a pleated skirt and two rows of buttons running up the front. She closed the trunk and stepped behind a stack of crates to try it on.

As the train approached Dover, she had suggested that they find a change of clothes in order to blend in more with the steamer passengers when they traveled to France. They felt guilty about taking things that didn't belong to them. But the circumstances required it.

"How about this for me?" Ozzie held up a black waistcoat with wide, pointy lapels and a matching vest.

"Posh," said Wiggins. "See if it fits."

Ozzie slipped the vest and coat over his own clothes.

"A little baggy, but they fit better than what you're wearin'," Wiggins said.

Ozzie dug around a bit more in the same valise until he located a shirt, tie, trousers, and boots. Before putting them on, he opened a matching valise and pulled out similar garments for Wiggins. "These bags must belong to two brothers," he observed.

"Just like us, mate," Wiggins said with a grin as he took the clothes. "Pilar, stay behind those crates until we call for you."

Swiftly, the boys changed clothes. The suit fit Wiggins perfectly, as did the boots. "I feel stiff and itchy," he complained.

"I guess fancy things don't agree with you," Ozzie said with a smirk. He pulled his tonic out of his old coat pocket and slipped it into his new one.

"I'm coming out now," Pilar called. When they saw her, the boys' mouths hung open.

"You look like a duchess," said Wiggins.

Ozzie smiled shyly. He'd never seen Pilar dressed so elegantly.

She twirled. "It's terribly dowdy, but I look like a proper girl. I won't stand out on the steamer. And neither will you two. You look like proper gents." Pilar glanced around. "Where shall we put our old clothes?"

"Search for Master's or Watson's valise. They must still be in here," Ozzie said. "They didn't have time to claim them."

After rummaging further, they found Master's bag and deposited their things into it. Ozzie pulled out one of Master's traveling hats with flaps and tried it on.

"Too large." Pilar laughed.

When Ozzie didn't respond, Wiggins nudged him with an elbow. "Oz, put it back."

"Right," Ozzie said absentmindedly, and complied.

Pilar and Wiggins exchanged a knowing look.

As the train pulled into Dover, they returned to the third-class carriage. Almost immediately, they observed a small train with one engine and two carriages chugging up the track and into the station behind them.

The three exited the train and stationed themselves by the ticket office. Before long, the small train entered the station and, as Ozzie expected, Moriarty and Moran stepped off.

While Moran headed to the telegraph office, Moriarty walked straight to the Continental Express. Passengers were still disembarking. Moriarty spoke with a conductor, who reviewed what appeared to be a manifest and bobbed his head. From there, Moriarty proceeded to the ticket office.

Ozzie, Wiggins, and Pilar turned their backs so as not to be observed.

"I guess we're goin' to France," Wiggins whispered without enthusiasm.

"Oui, oui," Pilar whispered happily.

*   *   *

Before they fully absorbed what they were doing, Ozzie, Wiggins, and Pilar stood on the deck of the steamer and watched the crew cast off. Just moments earlier, they'd spied Moriarty and Moran enter the first-class cabin.

"Excellent. They still think Master and Watson are on this ship." Ozzie smiled.

The closer we get to danger, the more alive he seems, Wiggins observed. "I still can't believe we're choosin' to follow the most dangerous men in all of England all the way to France — by *ourselves*." He'd hardly realized he'd said the words aloud until Pilar whispered, "It will be fun," and then signaled him to keep quiet and pointed to the first-class cabin door.

Wiggins turned to see Colonel Moran step onto the deck and walk toward them.

"He probably won't recognize Wiggins and me, but just in case . . ." Casually, Ozzie opened the door to the second-class cabin and motioned for Wiggins and Pilar to follow him.

They found seats in a crowded area of the cabin. Moran entered and walked up and down the aisle, scouring faces.

A *Sporting News* and a *Punch* magazine had been left on an empty seat beside the trio. Ozzie handed *Punch* to Wiggins and held up the *Sporting News* to hide his face and Pilar's.

"I've never 'ad more fun in me life," Wiggins whispered to Pilar.

CHAPTER TWENTY

STOWAWAYS!

The bearded man lay unconscious in the barn. After he and his large companion had been bound up with rope, Bloomfield questioned the driver, but all he would reveal was the other's name — Whitley.

The Irregulars waited outside for Jerry to return with the constable. Alfie and Barnaby played with Wiggins's ferret, Shirley. As all the boys spoke about their luck in capturing both men without anyone being injured, they heard the snort of a horse. Before they realized what was happening, Whitley came galloping past them on one of Bloomfield's mares.

Without thinking, Rohan climbed into Whitley's dogcart and slapped the reins. The horse lurched forward as Elliot jumped into the cart. Alfie handed Shirley to Barnaby, then ran after them and leapt in behind Elliot.

"Faster, Ro!" the boys yelled as they chased Whitley down the path and out of the farm.

Bloomfield and the remaining Irregulars stood watching in shock.

"Should we really chase 'im, or just let 'im ride off? I don't think we'll catch him."

Even though Whitley did not ride so well bareback, he was on a lone horse, while Rohan's horse had to drag a cart and three boys. Rohan did his best to keep Whitley in sight.

"Let's go after 'im. Otherwise he'll keep comin' after us. And he might lead us to Moriarty," said Alfie.

Elliot looked around. "It's pretty wide open 'ere. Whitley won't lose sight of us easily." But even as he said the words, he found himself longing to go back to the quiet of the farm and be done with this whole adventure. Maybe stepping up to fill Ozzie's and Wiggins's shoes was too much — or just not what Elliot wanted to be doing anymore. . . .

They followed the road back through town and continued east. A few times they lost sight of Whitley as they traveled through a small town, only to find him again on a country road. They trailed him into the port town of Newhaven, some fifteen miles from Haywards Heath. Then they lost him once more. Rohan drove the cart up and down the streets while Elliot and Alfie looked around without luck.

The boys agreed to go a short distance farther, toward the beach. On a hillside, they saw a fort, and in front of them, a wide swath of sand.

"Look!" Alfie said excitedly. "Let's stop and go for a swim. I never swum in the ocean before."

"We're workin' 'ere, Elf." Elliot tried to sound stern, but his words were not convincing to Alfie or even to himself. In truth, the beach and surf looked inviting. He hadn't seen the ocean since he'd arrived in England.

Rohan gazed out at the sea and shuddered. "We've lost 'im, and we don't know our way about." In truth, he, too, had had enough of this adventure and wanted to return to the farm. But then he thought of Wiggins asking him to take charge. He turned the cart back to town. "Maybe Whitley came to Newhaven to catch a boat. Let's investigate the docks."

Disappointed, Alfie and Elliot watched longingly as Rohan led them away from the beach.

The Newhaven harbor held a variety of boats: small rowboats, larger fishing boats, and vast cargo ships with masts as tall as trees and sails the size of buildings. The paddle steamer was the sleekest.

Fishermen and sailors filled the docks. Stevedores unloaded crates from ships. The smell of salt water and old fish was everywhere.

Rohan drove the cart slowly through the port while Elliot and Alfie scoured the area for Whitley.

After several laps around, Elliot looked at Rohan. "I guess we should go back to the farm."

Reluctantly, Rohan agreed. He was tense and tired and realized they would likely not find Whitley. Ignoring Alfie's pleas to return to the beach, he turned the cart back through town. Traffic and an impolite coach driver forced him to turn down a side street and pass through an area of clothing and dry goods shops.

"Ro!" Alfie said.

"Enough now, Elf. We're goin' back to the farm." Rohan's voice was filled with uncharacteristic impatience.

Alfie stood up in the cart and pointed at two gentlemen exiting a men's clothing shop, carrying carpetbags. "Look!"

Rohan slowed the cart to get a better view of the men. "Is that Master?" he whispered.

"And Dr. Watson," Elliot finished. "Do you see Ozzie or Wiggins? They're supposed to be trailin' 'em."

Rohan looked around and shook his head. "Elf, sit back down and crouch. Elliot, turn your back." Rohan gently slapped the reins and drove the cart down the street and around the corner, where he parked beside some delivery carts.

Elliot and Alfie followed Rohan as he climbed

down and peered around the corner where Holmes and Watson strolled.

"I still don't see Oz and Wiggins," he whispered.

The boys stepped into a doorway and watched Holmes and Watson pass. They waited a few minutes to see if Ozzie and Wiggins appeared.

When they didn't, Alfie said, "I hope they're all right."

"I don't get it," Rohan said. "Shouldn't Master and Dr. Watson be in Dover or on their way to France?"

Elliot stepped out into the street. "It looks like they're headed for that ship."

The boys watched them board the paddle steamer. Purposefully, Rohan started toward the dock. Elliot and Alfie followed.

"What are you thinkin', Ro?" Elliot asked.

"We told Oz and Wiggins we'd step up. They're not here. If somethin' has 'appened to 'em, we need to take over and shadow Master and Watson."

"Where do you think we're goin'?" Alfie asked.

"Across the channel. To somewhere in France or Europe. We'll find out soon enough."

Elliot watched a sailor checking passenger tickets on the gangway. "Any ideas on how we're goin' to board the boat?"

"I know a few things about ships. I grew up around 'em." Rohan's stomach twisted as he thought of going to sea. After what happened to his father, he was going to set out on a steamer?!

He took a breath and put on a brave face. "Boys, keep close to me."

CHAPTER TWENTY-ONE

OZZIE, WIGGINS, AND PILAR ARRIVE ON THE CONTINENT

The professor looks angry." Pilar could not contain her smile as she watched Moriarty stomp his foot.

"I guess he finally realized that Master was not on our steamer," Wiggins said.

After a smooth and uneventful voyage across the English Channel, they had arrived in the port of Calais, disembarked, and now stood in the crowd that had formed at the bottom of the gangplank.

"Pilar, can you tell what he's saying to Moran?" Ozzie asked.

Moriarty stood some fifty feet away, and Pilar strained to read his lips. "He just said something that would be impolite to repeat." She blushed and then turned serious. "Wait, something about some-one, I didn't get the name, and luck in Newhaven. And now he's saying they might as well take the train to Paris and pick up their search from there."

"Right," Ozzie said, pointing to the platform across the way and pulling out the pound notes that Master had given them. "We'll need tickets for the train."

Wiggins shook his head. "Oz, maybe we should stop spendin' so much. We don't know how long this trip is goin' to be."

"And besides, we need to get francs first," Pilar informed them. "Remember, we're not in England anymore." The boys just looked at her. Clearly, the need for foreign currency had not occurred to them.

A self-satisfied grin spread across Pilar's face. "It's all right," she assured them. "We'll find a bank in Paris. Any thoughts on how to get on the train, though?"

Ozzie looked at Wiggins, who looked at the wait-ing train and smiled confidently. "That I can do."

Chasing a moving train in their stiff new clothes and shoes was not easy, but Wiggins had insisted they wait until it began to pull away. The three managed to climb on the rear without being noticed. Fortunately, their destination, the baggage compartment — a tight, stuffy space with no windows — was also in the rear of the train. Once there, they dug around until they located Master's and Watson's luggage. Pilar had suggested that they claim one bag each in order to look like respectable travelers.

When Pilar heard the conductor announce that they were approaching Gare du Nord, she signaled the boys to follow. As the train slowed, they made their way nonchalantly through the adjacent carriage to an exit door. A few passengers gave them strange glances, and two boys laughed at Ozzie's and Wiggins's suits. Ignoring them, Pilar and the boys leapt onto the platform and plunged into the crowd.

The Gare du Nord, with its glass and iron structure, looked so different from the stations in London. Wiggins just stared. Around them, people in strange attire with unfamiliar faces hurried past, sometimes jostling them and muttering words Wiggins could not understand. He felt uncomfortable.

Meanwhile, Ozzie gazed back at the train, watching for Moriarty and Moran. He tried to anticipate what Moriarty would do next. But the whereabouts of Master and Watson kept distracting him — along with the fact that Watson was traveling *alone* with Master. How Ozzie wished that *he* could travel alone with Master.

As Pilar looked about at the elegantly dressed travelers, her heart burned, from joy or anticipation or longing, she could not tell. Too much time had passed since she'd been on the Continent. And suddenly she yearned for the adventure of the circus, and the diverse people, places, and customs that were once part of her everyday life.

While the three were engaged in their private

thoughts, Moriarty and Moran exited the train and proceeded to a phaeton carriage waiting for them outside the station. Ozzie motioned for Wiggins and Pilar to follow him as he waved down an old coach.

Ozzie opened the door and pointed to the phaeton. "Please follow that carriage."

The driver tilted his head as if asking a question.

"Suivez cette calèche, s'il vous plaît!" Pilar said, stepping past Ozzie and Wiggins and climbing inside.

"Oui, Mademoiselle," said the driver, and tipped his hat to her.

Ozzie smiled at Pilar admiringly. "Well done."

Wiggins seemed slightly dumbfounded. "You speak French?"

"Un peu. A little," she answered as the hackney followed the phaeton through the bustling city streets. When they reached the Hotel du Louvre on the Rue de Rivoli, Moriarty's carriage stopped, and he and Moran stepped out. The hackney slowed

behind them. Pilar noted the address and then called up to the driver to continue on and circle the block.

"Oh, look, the Jardin des Tuileries!" Pilar pointed to a long stretch of garden, brimming with lush tulips and daffodils. "Mamá took me here years ago, and oh, how I loved it. The Parisians were not always that kind to Gypsies, but inside the garden, it didn't matter. The flowers didn't care where we'd come from."

Pilar's thoughts were clearly far away, and Wiggins cleared his throat. "What are we doin'? It's nice to see the sights and all, but we're supposed to be trailin' the professor, remember?"

"Well, we couldn't very well get off our carriage in plain view of him, could we?" Pilar sounded defensive. "I thought we could circle their hotel while we decide what to do."

"She has a point, mate," Ozzie agreed.

"Thank you, Ozzie. Plus, I thought we could find a crepe cart. I'm starving."

Chastened by their logic, and heartened at the thought of food, Wiggins said, "I'm just sayin', we 'ave to stay focused. And we 'ave to do things different than at home. But a bite of food sounds grand."

Ozzie nodded. "You are right, mate. We need to stay close to Moriarty and Moran. But we don't have enough money to check into their hotel. And we would certainly stand out like old fish if we lounged on the sidewalk." Ozzie grew quiet for a moment. "Pilar, do you think you could direct our driver to a bank so we can pay him? Then we need to find a telegraph office."

CHAPTER TWENTY-TWO

CROSSING
THE CHANNEL

"Quick, before one of the deckhands sees us!" Rohan helped Alfie and Elliot out of the shipping crate filled with passenger luggage, where they had lain in utter discomfort for the past two hours. They had climbed in the container, unbeknownst to the crew, while it was still on the dock, and were loaded onto the paddle steamer amidst hundreds of trunks and suitcases. At last, Rohan felt it was safe to come out.

"Oh, me gut," Elliot complained. "I need fresh air." Queasy and light-headed, he stumbled around the cargo, lost his footing, and grabbed hold of the ship's railing.

"Keep the cargo between you and the cabin, mate, and maybe they won't spot us. You know what they do with stowaways."

Alfie's eyes grew large with concern.

Rohan smiled, even as he tried to sound serious. "They throw 'em overboard."

Elliot now hung over the railing, holding his stomach and moaning. "I'm gonna be *spotted*."

"Stitch, you look a bit green." Alfie snorted.

Elliot was too miserable to respond. "How much longer?" he managed to squeak out.

"Three hours, maybe more." Rohan's voice sounded far away amidst the hiss of the steam engine and the noisy churning of the paddles. "My father crossed the channel several times when he worked on the bigger ships — fishing boats, not steamers like this one. But he used to tell me how fast the steamers were. You can't see 'em now, but this one 'ere has electric lights."

Rohan poked his head around the crates and gazed at the main cabin, located on their deck, and the pilot tower on the upper deck. Now that they were out on the water, he felt better. "Imagine workin' on a ship. You could wake up each mornin' in a new place. Wouldn't that be somethin'?"

"Ugh." Elliot retched into the waves.

When darkness fell, Rohan and Alfie decided to investigate Holmes and Watson's whereabouts. Elliot had vomited four times, so they let him sleep nestled between several crates.

Electric lights illuminated the main cabin, the pilot tower, and the upper deck. Though the passengers remained in the cabins, crew members trolled the deck. Rohan and Alfie skulked in the shadows.

"Master and Dr. Watson may be in a private cabin below deck, or they could be dining in the main cabin," Rohan whispered, peeking through a porthole.

Alfie was too short to reach the small round window.

"Not that one." Rohan shook his head and moved them along to the next. They continued on until they reached the dining cabin. "There they are!" he said in a loud whisper. "The cabin is very grand. Looks like they finished dinner and are smokin' cigars. . . ."

"Lift me up, mate!" Alfie begged.

Rohan obliged.

"Oh, wow! That's a room fit for the queen."

As Rohan lowered Alfie, they heard footsteps on the stairwell to the lower deck. Quickly, they slipped into the darkness of the outer deck and waited.

A tall figure, wearing a suit and aided by a cane, emerged.

Before even seeing the thick beard, Rohan knew who it was. He placed a hand over Alfie's mouth.

As Whitley drew closer, Rohan and Alfie held their breath and watched him walk to the porthole that they had stared through just moments before.

Whitley mumbled something to himself, but the only words the boys could discern were "grander prey." They shuddered and waited for Whitley to return below deck. As they crept back through the shadows to rejoin Elliot, Rohan grew tense. Had

Whitley seen them stow away? Or was he following Master and Watson? Rohan had only wanted to step up and help, as Wiggins had asked. But was he making things worse?

The paddle steamer arrived at the port of Dieppe after ten P.M. Moments earlier, the boys had climbed back into the crate, which was lifted by a crane high into the air and deposited with a loud thump onto the dock. If not for the fact that his stomach was entirely empty, Elliot would have surely retched again.

Once the crew members began to unload the baggage, the boys scurried out onto the dock and searched the crowd for Holmes and Watson, all the while keeping vigil for Whitley.

Elliot walked silently and stepped gently, as if he were discovering his feet for the first time.

Around them, carriages filled the street, greeting passengers from the steamer. Alfie was teasing Elliot about his weak stomach when they saw Master and Dr. Watson climbing into a carriage.

Traffic moved slowly, and the boys — even Elliot in his fragile state — were able to follow on foot to the railway station, where Master and Watson disembarked and proceeded to a platform. Rohan peered around anxiously for Whitley. With his height and beard, he'd be easy to spot in a crowd. But he was nowhere in sight.

"Where do you think they're goin'?" Alfie asked.

Rohan looked at the words on the sign above Master and Watson's train. Ozzie had taught him to read a little, but these words were totally unfamiliar. "I think it's in French," he said, and noted track number three.

"I need some water," Elliot said calmly.

Rohan nodded, thinking that maybe Elliot wasn't up to anything besides sleep.

But then, Elliot surprised him. "Afterward, we need to find a way to board that train."

Though Rohan wished they could travel backward in time, before this whole adventure had started, he realized they had come this far and must finish the job. Right now, that meant trailing

Master and Watson. Swiftly, Rohan led the boys to a bathroom. Because of the hour, it was empty. While Alfie and Rohan relieved themselves, Elliot drank and splashed water on his face at a small white porcelain sink. It seemed to bring him back to life.

As soon as they exited the bathroom, a porter yelled words they did not understand. Instinctively, they tore across the station and down one of the train platforms. They jumped off the platform and ran down the tracks. After the boys had gone some fifty yards beyond the station, Rohan stopped and bent over to catch his breath. The others did the same. With darkness all around them and the porter nowhere in sight, they realized they were safe. They stood in a flat open area where ten sets of railroad tracks ran parallel to one another. An old wooden maintenance shed stood adjacent to the tracks.

Rohan looked back at the station, lit by the moon and dozens of lampposts. He located track three and the train Master and Watson had boarded.

"I'm hungry," Alfie complained.

"We all are," Rohan assured him. "But before we can scrounge some food, we have to catch Master's train as it passes."

Meanwhile, Elliot crossed the tracks to the shed. The door was open, and an array of tools hung on the wall, along with an old biscuit tin. Feeling better, Elliot took the tin from its hook and popped off the top, hoping to find some food. But inside were just a bunch of rusty nails.

Rohan and Alfie searched the shed for anything to eat, without luck. Rohan found a coil of rope on the floor and slung it over his shoulder. When he saw the train steaming in the station, he motioned the boys to get ready.

CHAPTER TWENTY-THREE

A SUITE AT THE HOTEL DU LOUVRE

In a luxurious sitting room of the Hotel du Louvre, hand-painted pastoral scenes danced across the walls: Meadows brimmed with delicate flowers, and lavishly dressed figures lounged in soft grass, sipping tea. The scenes were lit by a crystal chandelier, suspended over a low, marble coffee table. Overstuffed furniture in rich silks — lush blues, greens, and lilacs — surrounded the table. Two large windows, framed in floor-to-ceiling velvet drapes, offered picturesque views of the Louvre museum and gardens. Adjacent to the sitting room were three bedrooms, a study, and a dining room.

Having just finished an exquisite meal of turbot, asparagus, and roasted potatoes, Pilar reclined on the settee and drank her tea. "All it takes is a telegram and some nice clothes to have all of this? It seems a bit ridiculous. I don't even look like you two." She giggled.

Wiggins sat at an oak dining table in the adjacent room. "I think it's brilliant!" he said between mouthfuls of steak. "Oz, you are a genius."

Ozzie dipped a fat strawberry into a bowl of fresh cream and grinned. He sat across from Pilar in an overstuffed chair with his feet propped on the coffee table. The telegram he had sent to the manager of the Hotel du Louvre claimed to be from a high-ranking government official in England, announcing the unexpected arrival of his children. Due to a family emergency, it said, his children would be arriving alone, and as soon as the matter was resolved, along with certain affairs of state, his wife would be joining them. Though the man at the front desk had gazed upon the children somewhat suspiciously, he arranged for a bellman to escort them to one of the finest suites in the hotel.

"Let's not forget that our father *is* the chancellor

of England. Where is he, anyway?" Ozzie laughed and popped another strawberry into his mouth.

Wiggins couldn't ever remember seeing his friend enjoy food so much. "Who's the chancellor?"

Ozzie smiled mischievously. "I have no idea."

Pilar placed her cup in its saucer and set it down on the small table beside the settee. She had been in posh sitting rooms before — well, at least one, Elsa Hoff's — and in truth, she was no more comfortable here than she had been there. While she appreciated the finery and the pretty details, she certainly did not feel at ease, even reclining. The chair, though well padded, had little support. Pilar shifted uneasily. Wealthy people have strange ideas about comfort, she thought. "Yes, this is lovely, but now that we are here, what are we going to do?"

Ozzie turned businesslike and leaned forward in his chair. "Right. We know from our inquiries at the front desk that Moriarty is still here and has not informed anyone of plans to leave in the morning. I think it is safe to assume that he will be here for the night. We need to take turns sitting in the lobby watching for him and Moran. Undoubtedly, Moriarty will be using his contacts to locate Master and Watson. We have to be ready to follow when they depart."

Pilar nodded, eager to get to work. Seeing Ozzie act more like his old self made her happy. But then she remembered the conversation they'd started on the train. "Ozzie, something's bothering me. You never told us what happened in Oxfordshire and why you've not been yourself since you returned. What did you learn there?"

Wiggins looked up from his platter of food, grateful to Pilar for pressing Ozzie on the matter. He had continued to wonder about it, too.

Ozzie looked from one friend to the other and realized he had to tell them the truth. But would they think he was mad?

Wiggins could see he was laboring over something. "It's okay, mate, you can trust us."

Ozzie nodded and looked down at his hands. "I think Master could be my father," he blurted. He looked back up at his friends. Instead of rebuke, their faces showed openness and awe, mixed with understanding, as though the pieces to some large, jumbled puzzle had suddenly arranged themselves into a clear picture.

Though a thousand questions filled their heads, Wiggins and Pilar just sat quietly and waited for Ozzie to say more.

He explained about the photos of his mother and the articles about Master together in Great-aunt Agatha's trunk, as well as their overlapping time in Oxford, and of course, Ozzie and Master's physical resemblance. All the while, his friends nodded, as though it did make some kind of sense.

"You don't think I'm a complete fool then?" Ozzie asked tentatively.

Wiggins looked at him kindly. "There is logic to it, mate. And it explains your genius," he said with a smirk. "Imagine that, Sherlock Holmes as your father!"

"Why not just ask him?" Pilar said plainly. "Master would answer truthfully."

That was the point, Ozzie knew. If the truth was that Master was *not* his father, he didn't think he could bear it. What would he do then? But he just nodded. "You are right. I need to learn the answer."

The room grew quiet after that. No one knew what to say.

A sudden knock at the door made them all jump.

Had the hotel authorities discovered their ruse?

Gazing at the call buttons by the door, Wiggins remembered and said, "That must be the valet! I thought we could use a shoe shine. Come in," he called, removing his boots.

The hotel room had three call buttons: one for the waiter, one for the maid, and one for the valet. Wiggins had experimented with each and learned that when someone inside the room pushed a button, a light went on in the hall, which summoned the corresponding staff member.

The door to their room opened and the valet entered, bowed, and said, *"Bon soir."*

Wiggins walked over, handed him his boots, and asked that he return them in the morning.

The valet looked expectantly at Pilar's and Ozzie's shoes lined up by the door and was about to retrieve them when Pilar shook her head and declined the shine. Instead, she asked the valet in French to please send the waiter back for their dirty dishes.

"*Oui, oui,* Mademoiselle," he said kindly, and then departed.

Wiggins reclined on a sofa, put his hand on his stomach, and let out a satisfied "Aaaaah."

"You've grown accustomed to the high life quite quickly," Ozzie noted.

"The one thing I've learned, Oz, is you must take advantage of an opportunity when it's offered or you never get any enjoyment out of life. At any time, someone might realize we don't belong 'ere and we'll be makin' a dash for it. I don't want any regrets."

Pilar laughed. "You better hope that we don't have to dash before the valet returns your shoes."

CHAPTER TWENTY-FOUR

ON THE STREETS OF BRUSSELS

Rohan, Elliot, and Alfie rode the top of Holmes and Watson's train all the way from Dieppe to Brussels. Still famished from their journey, Rohan and Elliot had devised a plan: They tied the rope they'd found in the shed around Alfie's waist and lowered him down the side of the dining carriage as the train was moving, hoping he could reach in an open window to snatch some food. Unfortunately, it didn't work.

By the time the three arrived in Brussels, they were starved and chilled to the bone from their windy ride. To make matters worse, it started raining. The boys followed Holmes and Watson to their hotel, but had not seen Whitley since the steamer.

Had they managed to lose him back at the train station in Dieppe? Rohan prayed they had. It was enough to trail Master and Watson without having to worry about Whitley trailing them. Exhausted, hungry, and wet, they spent the night shivering in a dark alley filled with dustbins and discarded crates, holding splintered boards over their heads to protect them from the rain. Why were they even in Brussels? Elliot wondered before he drifted into a fitful sleep. Hadn't Wiggins said something about France?

The next day, the skies cleared, and they discovered an open-air market where they scrounged some potatoes, onions, and carrots before tracking Holmes and Watson through the city. They watched them buy clothing and additional luggage and then dine at a picturesque bistro. Thankfully, Whitley was still nowhere in sight.

That night, while Holmes and Watson again slept in the posh Metropole Hotel, the boys huddled together under a cart in the open-air market. They had spoken little that day. Each had wondered what had happened to Wiggins and Ozzie.

They were awakened the next morning by two

mongrel dogs that sniffed them curiously before trotting off. Still damp, and dirtier than usual, they made their way sleepily to Holmes and Watson's hotel. The boys kept vigil, peering through the wheel spokes of a carriage parked across the street.

"I need a good muffin," Alfie said dreamily.

"I'd be happy if my trousers would dry," said Elliot.

Rohan sat quietly, focusing on the hotel entrance. He felt responsible for Elliot and Alfie and wished he had done a better job keeping them fed and warm.

Moments later, Master and Watson exited the hotel and climbed into a carriage, which was being loaded with their bags.

"Now where are they going? We're just startin' to find our way around this place." Elliot sounded more tired than annoyed.

"I don't mind goin' somewheres else. We ain't done so well here." Alfie looked around. "But the buildings sure are somethin', like in a storybook."

Just as Holmes and Watson's carriage departed, Rohan hopped on the back of an enclosed delivery cart headed in the same direction. Alfie and Wiggins followed.

They were settling in for their ride when a tall man with a thick beard and sideburns exited the building across from the Metropole and hailed a cab.

Rohan groaned inwardly.

"You think he's been hidin' the whole time right above where we been loafin'?" Alfie asked.

Elliot nodded grimly. "He's likely been watchin' us *and* Master. We 'ave to be more careful."

When the boys' cart stopped, the three hopped off and followed Holmes and Watson's carriage on foot. They trailed them to another train station. Whitley had as well.

Stealthily, the boys weaved in and out of the crowd and tracked Holmes and Watson to a train headed to Strasbourg. A conductor yelled something they could not understand and then chased them out of the station.

"Do we stand out that much?" Rohan asked.

"We must," said Elliot. "We never 'ave this problem in London."

The boys turned to circle the station and head to the tracks from the opposite direction when Rohan, a few paces behind the others, felt a hand on his shoulder.

He was about to run when the grip tightened. Whitley, he thought, when he saw the boys' eyes grow wide.

Alfie squealed, "Master!"

Sherlock Holmes stood in his Inverness cape, looking exactly the same as he did in London.

"You boys have done quite a job of following us, but I cannot say I am pleased to see you. The train is about to depart, so step lively."

Elliot walked quickly to keep up. "Master, there's a man followin' you, too. The one that we saw outside of Dr. Watson's home two days ago. He's somewhere in the station, and 'is name is Whitley."

"With all the commotion your presence has caused, I am sure that the man of whom you speak is watching us at this very moment," Holmes said sternly.

The boys felt chastened by his cool response. Master remained silent during the entire time he booked passage and boarded the train. The boys trailed dolefully behind.

When the group arrived in the first-class car, Watson looked up from his newspaper at the boys and frowned. "However did you end up here? Holmes, you didn't summon these ragamuffins, did you? Where are the others?"

Holmes sat on the upholstered seat across from Watson and remained quiet, his expression unreadable.

"We do not know where our mates are," Rohan answered, straining not to let his voice crack. "Ozzie and Wiggins set out to follow you, but we 'aven't seen 'em since London."

"I certainly hope they stayed in England," Watson said, snapping open his newspaper and resuming his reading while muttering unintelligible words under his breath.

The engine whistle blew, the doors closed, and the boys slumped in their seats.

Still expressionless, Holmes stared out the carriage window. "The question is, What do we do with you now?"

CHAPTER TWENTY-FIVE

SURVEILLANCE AT THE HOTEL

The following morning, Ozzie sat in a velvet padded chair in the grand lobby of the Hotel du Louvre with a copy of the *Times* held up to his face. He read a few lines and glanced around. His surveillance the night before had revealed no signs of Moriarty or Moran, and now their arrival in the lobby felt imminent. Ozzie felt his pulse soar with anticipation as Pilar and Wiggins approached and sat in chairs opposite him. He lowered the paper to his lap.

"We just had a pleasant conversation with the doorman." Pilar's gaze traveled from Ozzie to the grand lobby entrance, and then back to Ozzie again.

"The professor and Moran are out for a walk," she continued. "They left some thirty minutes ago. They have a suite of rooms on the fourth floor. The main door is room 408. They received a telegraph message just before they departed."

"Pilar got all that by herself," Wiggins boasted. "The doorman didn't speak a lick of English. I don't know what she said, but he kept smilin' and noddin'."

Pilar flashed a smile. "He said I reminded him of his favorite niece."

Ozzie rose to his feet. "Excellent. Let's make a visit to room 408, shall we?"

The hallway was empty. Wiggins put his hands against the door and leaned forward so that Ozzie could hoist himself onto his shoulders, pull up his feet, and stand.

In spite of Ozzie's slight frame, Wiggins grunted from the effort. "We're just like the Zalindas, eh?"

Pilar stood lookout a few paces down the hall. "Hurry, the light just turned on for maid service in room 400."

Ozzie reached up to the transom and pulled. The window opened. He grabbed the corner of the frame with one hand and the encasement above the door with the other. Then he pulled himself through and lowered himself into Moriarty's sitting room. Once he was safely inside, he closed the transom by yanking back the chain.

As agreed, Pilar returned to the lobby to keep watch for Moriarty. Wiggins waited inside the service stairway and surveyed the hall.

Moriarty's vast sitting room contained an array of furniture but no personal effects anywhere. Ozzie approached the desk and saw a letter opener and, atop a small stack of papers, a telegram. It read: "SH in Brussels. Length of stay unknown. Advise. W."

Thoughts and questions fired in Ozzie's brain. The telegram had been sent that morning. Someone had followed Master to Brussels, but who? Who was W? Had Moriarty gone out to send a reply? Would Brussels be his next destination?

Think, Ozzie chided himself. Act like the great detective.

The papers beneath the telegram were train schedules. Seeing nothing else of interest in the sitting room, Ozzie proceeded to one of the bedrooms.

A suit hung in the closet above a pair of boots. Three suitcases remained mostly packed. Apart from the clothes and some grooming items, Ozzie found nothing of interest. He surmised that these belonged to Moran.

He reopened the largest case and noticed that it appeared deeper on the outside than on the inside. He rapped a knuckle on it, which produced a hollow sound. Feeling around the inside edge, he found a small lever. When pulled, a false bottom opened and revealed a rifle of sorts, in four pieces, along with a box of bullets.

The stock, trigger mechanism, bullet chamber, and barrel were each individually held in place with leather straps attached to the inside wall of the bag. A black ball was connected to the bottom of the bullet chamber. Ozzie touched it and realized it was made of rubber and trimmed in leather. He pushed it with a finger and air rushed out the metal loop affixed to its top.

Hadn't Master said that Moran attempted to shoot him with an air gun? Ozzie realized the ball must be the pump for the rifle, the part that gave it power.

Looking at the rifle, he felt anxious. He couldn't very well just leave it here, could he? Surely Moran would use it to try to shoot Master. Then again, if Ozzie took it, Moran and Moriarty would know they were being pursued. And Ozzie knew they could easily purchase another rifle.

Reluctantly, he decided to put it back. That was when he remembered the letter opener on the desk in the sitting room. He retrieved it and carefully punctured a small hole in the bottom of the rubber ball. He squeezed the ball and listened with satisfaction to the sound of air leaking out of it.

In the lobby below, Moriarty strode purposefully to the front desk, his cape swinging behind him like bat wings. Beside him, Moran moved with the sharpness of a soldier in his prime.

Immediately, Pilar turned toward the hallway that led to the service stairs. All she had to do was run up to the fourth floor and warn Wiggins, who in turn, would warn Ozzie. But before she had gone more than three paces, the hotel manager called to her.

"Mademoiselle, Mademoiselle, may I speak with you, *s'il vous plaît*?"

Pilar stopped, turned back around, and attached a smile to her face. "*Oui,* Monsieur?"

"Have you news of your father, his excellency the chancellor? We have had no other telegrams from his office, and it is my understanding that neither he nor your mother has been in contact with you. You have arrived here with no supervision. Strange, no? Our younger guests usually have custodians." The manager's tone was not entirely friendly.

Out of the corner of her eye, Pilar watched Moriarty and Moran cross the lobby and head toward the lift.

"Monsieur, my parents are extremely busy people. Their children have been raised to act independently. I hope you are not suggesting that their conduct toward us is in any way . . . inappropriate?" Pilar fixed the manager with a fierce stare.

Though still not convinced of her story, it was clear he did not want to offend a head of state, or even the daughter of one. "Of course not, Mademoiselle. I apologize if I have been misunderstood," he said with a slight bow. "We shall simply await your parents' arrival."

"Good. They'll be pleased to meet you, I am sure," Pilar said, looking again to the lift, where the doors were now closing with Moran standing inside. "I am certain Father will wish to speak with you directly." Pilar made sure her tone was sufficiently threatening. Then she headed past the manager, out of the lobby, and down the hall. The lift had begun to ascend.

Ozzie was surprised to find only one suitcase in Moriarty's room. It was made of black skin with a pattern he had never seen before. Was it alligator? Ozzie tried to open it, but some hidden tumbler system kept it locked. In the closet, he found only a light overcoat.

As he was leaving the room, he noticed a small frame on one of the nightstands. He stopped to get a closer look. Inside was a sketch of a small boy, maybe four years old, standing next to the curtain of a woman's skirt.

How odd, Ozzie thought. Did Moriarty have a son? Seeing the woman's skirt made Ozzie think of his mother for the first time in what seemed like ages. She hadn't died so long ago, not quite two years. He tried to picture her face, to hear her voice, but somehow, with the passage of time, that became more and more difficult. He swallowed back a lump in his throat as he set down the frame. He took one last look at the boy. Is that what I looked like when I was young?

Just then, two short raps sounded on the door to the sitting room. Ozzie recognized Wiggins's warning immediately and ran to the suite door and opened it. By now, Wiggins had already made his way down to the far end of the hall and was motioning for Ozzie to follow.

Ozzie paused, wondering if there was a way to lock the door behind him, when he heard the ring of the lift and saw a man exiting. He shot Wiggins a look and waved him on. Wiggins's eyes grew large and he shook his head. But Ozzie just stepped quietly back into the sitting room and locked the door behind him. He ran to Moriarty's bedroom, knowing it had its own door to the hallway, and waited until he heard someone enter the sitting room. Then he peeked out the bedroom door into the hallway and saw Moran close the main door to the suite. Relieved, Ozzie slipped out into the hall.

As he made his way to the service stairway, the bell to the lift rang again. He was standing right in front of the doors when they opened. To his horror, out stepped Moriarty. Before Ozzie could turn away, the professor clamped down on his shoulders with his talonlike fingers and stared straight into Ozzie's face.

"So, young man, we meet again."

CHAPTER TWENTY-SIX

HOLMES'S PLAN

If Holmes had decided what to do with Rohan, Elliot, and Alfie, he had yet to tell them when they arrived in Strasbourg later that Monday.

On the train, the boys had shared briefly their experiences in the days since they had last seen Master and Watson. When they described what had occurred with Whitley at Bloomfield's farm, Holmes interrupted.

"The man sounds like quite the bungler. I am surprised Moriarty would not have engaged some-one more seasoned — particularly when the stakes are so high." He stroked his chin. Though he lis-tened to the boys until they finished their tale,

Holmes spent the rest of the trip staring out the window, deep in thought.

Other than marveling at the fact that Rohan and company had been following them for two days undetected, Watson did not speak much either. The boys were uncomfortable with the silence. But they accepted it graciously in exchange for a bountiful breakfast in the dining carriage.

After they arrived at Strasbourg Station, they hailed a cab and rode directly to the hotel. None of them observed Whitley along the way.

A telegram awaited Holmes at the hotel desk. As soon as they were shown to their room and the bellman had departed, he read it, all the while pacing and nodding.

"Well, Watson, my net has been pulled in. Scotland Yard reports that all of Moriarty's organization has been arrested, though they haven't found Moriarty himself. Of course, it does not surprise me that they seem to be unaware of Moran and this fellow Whitley."

Rohan watched Holmes remove his clay pipe from his coat pocket and pack the bowl full of tobacco. It was a relief to be with him. In spite of his sometimes brusque manner, Master would protect and feed the boys, and Rohan felt thankful for that.

"Undoubtedly, Whitley has been in communication with Moriarty, which might be quite useful." Holmes puffed on his pipe and paced the room.

Though grateful for the food and shelter, Elliot found himself again wishing he'd stayed on Bloomfield's farm. He wanted to learn about cattle, work in the pastures, and explore the forests. This whole trip seemed like a failure.

Elliot studied the great detective with a bit of annoyance. He found Master's tendency to make a statement and then sink into thought without regard to others rather rude. The man was a genius, to be sure, but he was also a difficult person. Elliot thought of his own father, who may not have been the most successful man in their village, but had friends everywhere he went. He realized he would much rather be like that than like Master.

For his part, Alfie had become quite bored. He wished he was traveling with just Rohan and Elliot.

Adults were fine for giving you things, but they were not much fun otherwise. He wouldn't mind sleeping in the streets again, even in the rain, if it could be just him and his mates.

Holmes exited his thoughts and addressed the boys again. "Moriarty must be aware by now that he no longer has an organization. This fact will only make him more vengeful. The time is right to set a trap for him. With the help of you boys and this Whitley fellow, we may succeed."

"Whitley will *help* us?" Rohan asked.

A smile formed on Holmes's lips as he puffed his pipe and rubbed his hands together. "But of course."

CHAPTER TWENTY-SEVEN

MORIARTY'S INTERROGATION

Moriarty stood in the center of the sitting room and read a telegram aloud to Ozzie and Moran. It reported that Holmes and company had left Brussels and arrived in Strasbourg.

"We need to leave Paris immediately!" Moran said.

But Moriarty shook his head. "We should wait." He did not explain why.

Later that afternoon, a second telegram arrived, this one from Moriarty's barrister. It informed him that arrests had been made, not just in London, but throughout England. Scotland Yard had raided Moriarty's vast network of associates simultaneously — the arrests orchestrated with such precision that his entire enterprise had been taken off the street.

Moran let out a passionate string of profanities, some of which Ozzie had never heard before.

While Moriarty paced the room, Ozzie sat on a settee and watched the professor's face contort into an outraged grimace, only to recede into an unemotional stare.

After a lengthy silence, Moriarty uttered a single word in a venomous whisper: "Holmes."

Ozzie felt the skin tighten around his neck.

The last twenty-four hours in Moriarty and Moran's company had passed slowly, in the haze of an unpleasant daydream. Ozzie rubbed his shoulder, still sore from Moriarty's grip the day before, and recalled the questions the professor had launched at him.

"Holmes has sent you, has he not?"

"No."

"Have you attempted to communicate with him?"

"No."

"Does he know that you are here?"

"No."

"Then why *are* you here?"

"I've been following you . . . to Master." As soon as Ozzie had answered the last question, he realized he'd been too quick to respond; he hadn't considered the consequences.

"To warn him?"

Ozzie paused and nodded.

"Are you alone?"

"Yes."

Moriarty's penetrating eyes bore into Ozzie's. "That is your first lie. Make it your last."

Ozzie felt his breath catch in his throat. Instinctively, he reached into his pocket for his tonic and realized he'd left the little that remained back in his suite. He took a deep breath and tried to hold back a coughing fit. Moriarty had seen through him too easily.

Moriarty had continued his interrogation, often repeating the same questions, or rephrasing them until he appeared satisfied. Occasionally, he would just sit in the stuffed chair across from Ozzie and gaze at him intently, as if reading his innermost thoughts.

Can he actually see inside my mind? Ozzie had wondered. Logically, he knew this couldn't be true, but still, it felt that way.

All the while, Moran sat casually at the desk, cleaning his nails with the blade of an ivory-handled pocketknife or staring menacingly at Ozzie. At one point, he asked, "Shall I take care of him, Professor?"

Ozzie shuddered.

But Moriarty had shaken his head. "I know this boy. Other than being mixed up with the wrong employer, he has, on occasion, shown promise. He shall remain with us for now."

"Professor, do we really have time for this urchin?"

Moriarty ignored the question.

"What about the others with him?" Moran pressed, still holding the knife.

"Ah, yes." Moriarty turned from Moran to Ozzie. "That is where we shall reach our first agreement. Young man, cooperate with me, and your friends shall suffer no harm. Fail to cooperate, and they shall suffer greatly. Do you understand?"

Ozzie nodded and accepted the terms.

Moriarty had then arranged for a letter on official stationery to be delivered to the hotel management, purportedly from the office of the English ambassador to France, warning of a threesome masquerading as the children of the chancellor of the English courts. The letter further indicated that the children were frauds. Ozzie did not know whether Wiggins and Pilar had been handed over to the Parisian police or simply tossed out of the hotel. But a day had passed without any sign from his friends.

Moriarty shredded the second telegram and sat in quiet contemplation. He did not smoke, or move around the room, or read a newspaper. The silence was a torment.

Moran announced that he needed some air and stepped out. Ozzie tried to read an old newspaper, but the words just blurred together. What does

Moriarty really want with me? he wondered. I do not know Master's plans. Moriarty understands his methods better than I do. What can I possibly offer him?

While Ozzie slipped into a trance, Moriarty broke out of his.

"You worked for Crumbly the forger," he said. "You were his best. Do you still use your talents?"

Ozzie snapped alert. "I have no reason to anymore."

"It is a waste, my boy, not to exercise your abilities. You'll find that if you don't, you may end up working at jobs less than suitable for you, while your true talents decline."

Ozzie considered Moriarty's counsel. In spite of the professor's wicked demeanor, something about his words felt good. No one, apart from his grandfather, who had died when he was a young boy, had ever advised him about life. Still, Ozzie did not plan to devote himself to being a forger.

"Tell me about *The Stuart Chronicle*. You spent much time alone with the book. Did you ever learn its secrets?"

Ozzie felt a strange pull to disclose the treasure hidden inside the book. He studied Moriarty, whose gaze emanated both coolness and warmth. What was it about him that drew Ozzie in?

Ozzie described the book's illustrations and the lavish script handwriting.

Moriarty raised an eyebrow. "That is all you recall?"

"I was tired while copying it," Ozzie lied.

"Describe the Temple of Diana then."

Ozzie closed his eyes and tried as best he could to explain the temple, its mosaics, and the gold statue.

Moriarty listened intently. "The accounts in the papers were imprecise at best. You have a scrupulous eye and excellent recall, my boy."

Inside, Ozzie tried to reject the compliment. This man was a thief and a murderer, after all. And yet, Ozzie could feel the lure of Moriarty's attention and appreciation. Though Master praised him from time to time, his mind was nearly always somewhere else.

A meal arrived, and Moriarty insisted that

Ozzie join him. While they ate, Moriarty continued to question Ozzie, even going so far as to inquire about his relations.

"I have none," Ozzie replied plainly.

"I have two brothers," said Moriarty, studying Ozzie with great curiosity. "Apart from them and their families, I am alone. My work has been my primary relation." Moriarty's voice seemed to soften.

Ozzie was surprised by how open the professor was. Why is he sharing personal information with me? Ozzie wondered. Should I have told him about Great-aunt Agatha and the possibility of a father somewhere?

Ozzie's thoughts were thus occupied when Moran returned and joined them at the table. Evening came, and with it a third telegram. Moriarty read it and told them that Holmes had boarded a train in Strasbourg headed for Geneva.

"Well?" said Moran.

Moriarty stood and started for his room. "Now it is time to follow."

CHAPTER TWENTY-EIGHT

MORIARTY'S SECRET

I t was late when they appeared at Gare du Nord. The station was empty except for a small crowd that gathered near their train. As they boarded, Ozzie saw an opportunity to flee from Moriarty and Moran, but he let it pass. Why had he done that?

He told himself that he was helping Master. Master's brother, Mycroft, had said that the surest way to aid Master was to trail Moriarty. By traveling with him, Ozzie was following as closely as possible, wasn't he? Inside, Ozzie knew the answer was more complicated.

What is it about Moriarty that intrigues me so much? he wondered.

Like Master, the man appears to be thinking

intensely at all times. A small suggestion, a slight fact, opens a world of information to him. Whenever he asks questions, there is a reason behind them. But unlike Master, Moriarty has a softness about him. He isn't gentle, exactly, but he is attentive and interested. Still, the man is a *criminal*, Ozzie reminded himself.

Ozzie's mind wrestled with all these details as he sat opposite Moriarty on a comfortable uphol-stered seat in the private first-class compartment. Moriarty's eyes were closed. His hands lay clasped in his lap. He appeared to be in a state of medita-tion rather than sleep. Beside him, Moran dozed. He'd already made several jaunts out of the carriage for a walk. Ozzie couldn't tell if he was restless or checking to see if they were being followed.

Exhausted, Ozzie tried to sleep. He nodded off now and again, but always jerked awake after a few minutes, worrying about his friends. What had happened to Wiggins and Pilar? He'd asked Moriarty back at the hotel, but he just deflected the question and assured him they were unharmed.

Ozzie had half expected — or perhaps just naively wished — they'd be waiting for him at the train station, but he hadn't seen them anywhere.

Ozzie's thoughts turned to Master. Can I really help him? What will I do when he and Moriarty meet? Will he think I've betrayed him?

"Plotting something, are you?"

Ozzie looked up to see Moriarty staring at him, a small grin playing at the corners of his mouth. Moran had gone for another walk, and they were alone in the compartment.

Ozzie shook his head and looked down at his fingernails, which were badly in need of a trim. "I'm just tired, that's all."

"You are a thinker who cannot shade his thoughts. What are we to do with you, my boy?"

"Send me back to England?" Ozzie offered a weak smile.

"Back to the streets of London? That would be a terrible waste. You have talents, my boy, talents that have not been properly utilized. Perhaps you will allow me to assist you in developing them."

Ozzie felt his chest squeeze, from fear or excitement he could not tell, but he thought it might be the latter. How would Moriarty have an opportunity to help me? He and Master will have a meeting of some kind, a final battle. Moriarty will end up in jail or dead. Or he might get away. Or —

"You are not listening to me, are you?"

Ozzie looked up and realized that Moriarty was still speaking to him. Instead of answering, Ozzie asked something he had been wondering about for days. "Who is that drawing of? The one in the frame on your nightstand in the hotel."

"I had forgotten that your real occupation is snooping." Moriarty's sharp tone made Ozzie flinch. But then Moriarty relaxed and took a breath. "That is a child I once knew . . ." He rubbed his hands, as if washing them. "He is my son."

Ozzie's eyes grew wide. Moriarty had a son? Hadn't he said he had no other relations besides his brothers and their families?

The train wheels screeched along the track. Moriarty stared out the window into the passing night. A muscle in his neck twitched.

Ozzie watched him methodically rub his hands some more and dared to ask, "Where is your son now?"

Moriarty continued to stare out the window. "I was married once, to a simple but honest woman. I had worked as a professor for many years. Then my business evolved and took me away more and more from my academic duties. I saw less of my family. My wife grew weary of my absences. In truth, I suspect she disapproved of my endeavors. And then, on my boy's fifth birthday, I arrived home with a clockwork train set only to find that they were gone." Moriarty's voice broke up on the last words and he forced a cough.

Ozzie waited for him to continue. When he didn't, Ozzie whispered, "Did you look for them?"

Moriarty slammed a fist on his armrest and glared at Ozzie. "Of course, I looked for him!"

Ozzie gasped and braced himself for a lashing.

But Moriarty just closed his eyes and rubbed his forehead. "I never found him. . . . With all my resources, I never found him."

CHAPTER TWENTY-NINE

A GATHERING
IN GENEVA

Whitley met them at the train station in Geneva. After shaking Moran's hand, he gazed at Ozzie and then approached Moriarty.

Ozzie could not believe he was standing so close to the bearded man who had tried to slash his friends with a sword! He averted his gaze.

"Good afternoon, Uncle. Why is this urchin with you?"

"Let's not dally, Whitley. Have you arranged a carriage?"

Ozzie looked up. This man was Moriarty's nephew? He must be the son of one of Moriarty's brothers. A cousin to Moriarty's lost son. Ozzie felt his chest burn all over again for Moriarty's sad tale.

Whitley pulled his beard sheepishly. "Well . . . no. I assumed we could take a cab."

Moriarty grimaced.

"But I do know where Holmes is, and I have learned his plans," Whitley said, attempting to regain his composure.

"Help the colonel find our bags," Moriarty said sharply, and then turned to Ozzie. "Master Manning, follow me."

On the carriage ride from the train station to the old section of Geneva, Whitley shared what he'd learned about Holmes: He had rented a house in Geneva under an alias and planned to stay for a week. During that time, he would continue to use his contacts to locate Moriarty, and would then inform the authorities.

Moriarty listened intently to Whitley, but remained expressionless. "How did you learn of Holmes's plans?"

Whitley flashed a proud smile. "I overheard

a conversation he had with Dr. Watson on the train. The three boys traveling with him left their carriage compartment door open a crack. I happened to be in the aisle of the train and stopped to listen."

Three boys traveling with Master? Ozzie realized they must be Irregulars! But who? And how did they end up with Master?

Moriarty gave his nephew a look that told him to continue.

"No one met them at the train station and no one greeted them at the house," Whitley said as the carriage drove slowly past a three-story stone house on a narrow cobblestone street just off the Rue Saint-Léger. Whitley pointed to it, and Moriarty and Moran studied it through the darkened carriage windows.

"What time did they enter that building?" Moriarty pressed Whitley.

"About two hours ago."

"That doesn't leave much time for them to have planned anything." Moran looked out the back window at the building and then at Whitley. "Did they see you follow them here?"

"Absolutely not," Whitley stated confidently.

Moriarty shook his head in disgust. "I believe Holmes has planned something and used you in the process.

"People do not learn information from Sherlock Holmes by accident, by eavesdropping. The man is a meddler, but not a fool. Look at that street." Moriarty pointed to where they had just been. "A pushcart at each end would be enough to barricade it and prevent escape. We just took a tremendous risk riding past that house. I allowed it because I am sure we are not being followed presently.

"Nephew, I realize your father is a stationmaster, and not one of us. But if you want to be part of our world and assist, you must be more careful."

Whitley stared down at his hands.

"What are we to do now, Professor?" Moran asked.

"Sherlock Holmes wishes to trap me and bring me to justice — *his* notion of justice. I have another idea, a compromise of sorts, but it will require direct contact."

Moriarty looked at Moran and Whitley. "The three of us cannot chance the meeting." Then he turned to Ozzie. "But maybe Master Manning here can put his great talents to use and serve a purpose for the benefit of all."

CHAPTER THIRTY

A MEETING
WITH HOLMES

Watson opened the door to the stone house. "Osgood? I certainly did not expect to see you here! Though, after the adventures your mates have had, I suppose it shouldn't surprise me. However did you find us?"

Ozzie managed a smile but did not know how to answer.

Watson held the door open, motioned Ozzie inside, and then checked the street before closing the door behind him. Inside, the rooms were cold and sparse with little furniture. Watson led Ozzie to a back room where Master reclined on a settee, puffing his pipe.

"Osgood, I anticipated we would be seeing you on this trip, but not quite in this way." Holmes examined Ozzie's new clothing with some amusement. "Your friends are upstairs resting."

"Who?" Ozzie asked awkwardly.

Holmes turned his head slightly to the side, like a bird, in contemplation. "Rohan, Elliot, and Alfie."

"Have you seen Pilar and Wiggins?" Ozzie asked.

Holmes shook his head.

Ozzie looked down at his feet. "I have been sent . . ." he started. He gazed up briefly and could see that he had Master's full attention.

"Yes, Osgood?"

"I have been sent by Professor James Moriarty — to deliver a message to you personally."

"Good heavens!" exclaimed Watson.

Ozzie had thought he could approach the matter straightforwardly when Moriarty explained his plan to call a truce. But as the carriage had drawn closer to Master's rented house, Ozzie suddenly realized that conducting himself that way might make him appear disloyal to Master. Standing before him now, Ozzie decided to deliver the offer as formally and as close to Moriarty's own words as possible. He hoped this would show Master that he wasn't choosing sides, but acting as a conduit of information. Master knew Moriarty's methods. Surely he would understand.

"The professor urges an accord, as an end to this matter. You have destroyed his organization and rendered him powerless. He will accept his premature retirement if you will accept yours. There is an alternative to mutual destruction. And the professor does not wish to spend the rest of his life wondering if he is being followed. He assumes that you do not wish that either. An armistice is in everyone's interest."

"My goodness, Holmes, the boy has joined Moriarty! The audacity — after all you have done for him." Watson's face flushed red with rage.

Ozzie felt his stomach churn. When Moriarty had described his plan, Ozzie thought it was a good one. But now he wasn't sure. Could they part ways on fair terms? If there was any chance, Ozzie wanted to help. Maybe then Master could return to London, satisfied that Moriarty was finished, and Moriarty could put his energy into finding his son.

Holmes puffed his pipe quietly and gazed out the window. The look in his eyes was so faraway that he might have been staring out across all of Geneva, maybe all of Switzerland. "Are those your words, Osgood?" he asked in a measured tone.

"I have repeated the professor's message to the best of my ability."

"How long have you been in Moriarty's company?"

"This is the fourth day."

Holmes nodded and turned to face Ozzie. "Where is the professor now?"

"I know only that he is traveling in a carriage around the city."

"Moran and Whitley are with him?"

Ozzie nodded.

"How are you to rejoin them?"

"There is a carriage waiting for me at the Place

du Bourg-de-Four. I do not know where it will go once I get on."

"You do not need to return to them, you know." Holmes's eyes were uncharacteristically soft, and his tone was kind.

"Osgood, did you hear me?"

Ozzie nodded, suddenly feeling foolish. Here he stood before the world's greatest consulting detective — a man who devoted his life to solving crimes and protecting the citizens of England, who had helped Ozzie himself by providing food and money and work, who was offering to help him yet again. And Ozzie was trying to foster an accord between him and the Napoleon of Crime!

Ozzie gazed down at his feet. Wasn't there some way he might still be able to help? Then he recalled Mycroft's advice. He managed a whispered reply. "I think I must."

"Do you know what to tell him, or should I give you my words?"

Ozzie kicked at a ball of dust. A lump formed in his throat. "I know what to say."

Holmes stood and set down his pipe. He strode over to Ozzie and put a hand on his shoulder. He had never done such a thing. "Are you up to this, Osgood?"

"Yes, sir," Ozzie sighed. He could not bring himself to meet Master's gaze. His pulse raced. He felt as if all of this were happening to someone else.

"Is there more, Osgood?" Holmes asked.

"Yes, I wish we were back in London."

Holmes smiled sympathetically. "I am afraid we are too far along for that."

"Yes, sir."

Holmes patted Ozzie's shoulder. "You have been an asset to my organization. I thank you for that." Holmes nodded a good-bye. "Good luck to you, my boy."

Ozzie felt tears spring to his eyes and immediately tried to blink them away. Though a million thoughts collided in his brain, all Ozzie could manage to say was, "And to you, Master."

During the entire exchange, Watson sat listening and looking puzzled. But he remained quiet.

It was a relief to leave. Ozzie stepped into the hallway, only to see Rohan, Elliot, and Alfie crouched on the stairs, silently watching him. How much had they heard? Did *they* think he was a traitor? He wanted desperately to stop and explain, but what would he say? His head felt filled with fog. The carriage was waiting for him. There was no time. And as Master said, they were too far along now.

Ozzie opened the door and gave a quick glance back at his friends. Alfie raised a hand and waved. Ozzie nodded and closed the door behind him.

Outside, in the chill air, beneath a dark, unforgiving sky, he bent over and retched.

CHAPTER THIRTY-ONE

OZZIE
REJOINS MORIARTY

The carriage left Ozzie beside a stretch of shore-line on Lake Geneva. He gazed up at the starless sky and waited. After a few minutes, he heard the rumble of a motor launch, and then a small light bobbed across the water. Moriarty steered the launch alongside a pier so Ozzie could board.

Though the Geneva police had attempted to follow him back to Moriarty, Ozzie's carriage was too fast.

As Moriarty steered the boat diagonally across the lake, Ozzie reported that Holmes had refused to compromise. In the dim moonlight, he could see Moriarty nod as though he had expected as much.

"I trust you delivered the message as directed,"

Moriarty said. His tone was one of confidence, not doubt.

"Yes, sir."

"Well done, my boy. I suppose our options have now been whittled down to one."

Why was Moriarty praising him, Ozzie wondered, when he had not succeeded in getting Master to agree to his terms? And what option was he referring to?

Moments later, they arrived at a small dock, where Moran waited with a bicycle.

"Holmes and company departed with their bags, along with the local authorities, almost immediately after the boy left the residence," Moran said. "They must be headed to the train station."

The two men removed their luggage from the launch and boarded a carriage that had been prearranged. When they arrived at the train station, Moran exited, proceeded briskly inside, and then returned to the carriage.

"They have boarded the 9:10 for Leuk. The engine is already fired up. The police are still in the station."

Moriarty nodded. "Holmes deals with the authorities only when necessary. Because he had hoped to trap us in Geneva, the authorities were useful to him. Now he no longer needs them. I am sure there are no police on the train. Did you see Whitley?"

Moran shook his head.

Moriarty said nothing, but his expression reflected annoyance. "I am sure he has followed them on. We should follow as well."

A train whistled and steam rose above the station.

"That's their train now," said Moran. "It's too late to board."

"Only by traditional means." Moriarty smiled. "Fortunately, I anticipated that might happen." He directed the carriage to a nearby stable, where three horses awaited them. They left their bags at the stable with instructions to hold them until further directed. From one of his bags, Moran removed a small rucksack, which he pulled over his shoulders. Then he and Moriarty mounted their horses. Ozzie, who had never ridden before, awkwardly hoisted himself up into the saddle.

"Now!" yelled Moran, and the three tore out of the stable after the train.

While Moriarty and Moran galloped effortlessly along the tracks, Ozzie bounced out of the saddle and up the horse's neck. He righted himself and slid back onto the saddle only to have the same thing happen again.

The train had steamed out of the station, and its speed was still building when Moran rode alongside the last car. With the grace of an acrobat, he stood up in his stirrups, brought his left leg over the saddle, stepped onto the edge of the small platform at the rear of the train carriage, and pulled himself over the rail. Moriarty followed and, with surprising agility, performed the same feat as Moran. Their horses ran off, away from the tracks.

The two men stared down at Ozzie, who continued to have trouble galloping and keeping up with the train. Moran waved him on. For one brief moment, Ozzie wondered what they would do if he turned his horse around, returned to the station, boarded a train to France, and booked passage back to England.

But now Moriarty was waving, too, and shouting words of encouragement. Ozzie slapped the reins and bounced in his saddle. His horse picked up speed. The next thing he knew, Moran had grabbed hold of the back of his jacket and lifted him off the horse while Moriarty assisted in pulling Ozzie onto the platform. Once atop, he gave Ozzie a pat on the shoulder.

Still panting from the effort, Ozzie followed the men into the train. They proceeded down the aisle and through the third-class, second-class, and dining carriages without seeing Whitley or Holmes and the others. They continued down the aisle to the first-class carriage and peered through the windows of the private compartments.

At last, they found Whitley, who appeared to be asleep with his head turned to face the outside window. Moriarty's jaw clenched as he slid open the compartment door. "What are you doing?" he hissed as he grabbed Whitley's shoulder and yanked him around to face him.

Whitley let out a groan. His wrists were bound behind his back, his ankles tied together with rope. And he had been gagged with handkerchiefs. He appeared groggy, but still conscious.

Moriarty reached back to close the compartment door and then removed the gag. With a flick of a large pocketknife, Moran cut the ropes.

Whitley rubbed the back of his head. "They surprised me. They hit me with something, and I came to in here. That's all I remember."

Moriarty looked at Moran, who exited the compartment and returned a few minutes later, his face a dark red. "Apparently, Holmes is not on the train, nor are the others."

Moriarty removed his top hat and sat down. He looked from Whitley to Moran. Then he closed his eyes and said in a defeated tone, "I travel with fools."

CHAPTER THIRTY-TWO

INTO THE ALPS

Wiggins wondered where Ozzie might be. It was Saturday, almost a week since Moriarty had caught him coming out of his hotel room, and three days since his meeting with Master in Geneva. Was Moriarty holding Ozzie by force? Or had Ozzie betrayed Master and the gang, as Watson had suggested? The latter thought so upset Wiggins that he tripped on a tree root and stumbled. Pilar caught him by the arm and kept him from landing on his face.

As they hiked along, Pilar remembered the kind doorman she had befriended at the Hotel du Louvre. If he hadn't warned them, she and Wiggins surely would have been arrested by the Parisian police and been trapped inside a cold jail cell right now instead of walking in this glorious Swiss wilderness.

After a narrow escape from the hotel, she and Wiggins had hidden out on the streets for a day and waited for Ozzie to emerge from the hotel with Moriarty and Moran. They then followed them to the train station and spent a long ride in a stuffy luggage compartment all the way to Geneva, where they tracked Ozzie to his meeting with Master. Why had Ozzie looked so distraught after emerging from the house Master had rented? Pilar wondered. He'd ridden off so quickly that Pilar and Wiggins had lost sight of him. It was a relief to meet up with Rohan, Elliot, and Alfie, not to mention Master and Watson.

As they hiked, Pilar thought of the bits of conversation the boys had overheard between Master and Ozzie, and found the whole thing hard to believe. Ozzie thought Master was his father. He wanted to be just like him. Why would he betray him and join Moriarty's organization?

In front of her, Wiggins, still unaccustomed to

the rugged terrain, stumbled again, then brushed himself off and kept on.

"Too much bratwurst in your gut, boss?" Alfie asked with a smile.

Elliot chuckled. He was panting from the exertion, but still, it felt good to be outside, in crisp clear air, surrounded by beautiful mountains.

They'd departed that morning from Leukerbad and were hiking up to the Gemmi Pass.

Rohan was assisting Dr. Watson, who walked with a slight limp and kept calling himself an "old campaigner." Rohan worried that he might not make it through the Alpine trek.

At the front of the line, Master strode energetically behind the guide. He wielded a staff to help him maneuver the steep terrain, and he whistled a tune.

Wiggins's thoughts turned momentarily to Pilar, who now walked ahead of him alongside Alfie. He realized he would not have made it this far without her. Her knowledge of languages and geography had kept them on track. Even when Master had tried to leave them all behind in Geneva and then again outside of Leuk, it was Pilar who convinced him that they would continue to follow him so he should just accept their company.

"I perceive your insistence on 'protecting me' will only place all of you in danger," he had said. "But I accept. I suppose you will be safer *with* me than following me." Here Master had paused to examine Pilar and the boys, and then said with a smirk, "What a motley band we make."

None of them had any idea where Moriarty, Moran, and Ozzie were. The last they had seen of them, they were chasing down and boarding the train for Leuk.

It was Master's idea to make their way leisurely to Leuk. Were they maintaining a safe distance behind Moriarty, or were they chasing him? Wiggins wondered. Whatever Master's plans, Wiggins hoped they would soon be heading home to England. He had had enough of "the Continent."

They hiked all morning. The Gemmi Pass was still deep in snow, though the trail was clear and patches of stone and green grass poked through here and there. Before they reached the summit, they came upon a mirrorlike lake bordered by stones and jagged cliffs. The party paused to admire a particularly breathtaking view.

"Ah, the Daubensee." Watson sighed with appreciation.

Just as they were all catching their breath and taking swigs from their waterskins, Wiggins heard a rumble overhead.

"Out of the way!" Holmes yelled as he pushed Elliot, Rohan, and Watson off the path and into a small gully. Wiggins dove, pulling Pilar and Alfie with him into a stone crevice.

From their various perches, they watched a boulder tumble down from a ridge above them and careen off the trail where they'd all been standing just seconds before. With a loud splash, it plunged into the lake.

Wiggins walked cautiously back to the trail, gazed up at the ridge, and back down at the jagged dent the boulder had left in the trail.

"I think they have found us," he said quietly.

CHAPTER THIRTY-THREE

OZZIE PROBES WHITLEY

Moriarty had led them back and forth through the Alps for three days. Ever since Master had tricked them onto the train to Leuk, Ozzie had watched the professor grow more compulsive. He behaved as if Master had spies in every village. He paid villagers to act as informants, giving strict instructions to search out two Englishmen traveling with a group of ragamuffin children.

Much to Ozzie's frustration, Moriarty withdrew more and more. When he remembered Ozzie was with them, he continued to treat him kindly. But Ozzie still had no idea what the professor's next move would be. He confided solely in Moran. It seemed they had reached the end of the game, Ozzie observed. But how would it unfold? And once the game was over, would anyone be left standing?

If only Ozzie could be left alone to think! But he was forced to share rooms at inns with Whitley and to take meals with him, too. Ozzie's ears rang from his endless monologues, in which he mumbled complaints about his uncle or vague threats toward Ozzie.

One morning, Moriarty left Ozzie and Whitley in the town of Frutigen while he and Moran rode south in a dog cart. They were instructed to remain in their rooms at the inn and not to venture out for any reason.

Around noon, Whitley began to pace. "Why don't we go into the village for some lunch?" The friendly tone of his voice caught Ozzie off guard.

"The professor told us not to go out," Ozzie reminded him.

"I am sure he meant we could eat."

"Yes, but I think he meant at the inn's dining room."

Whitley exhaled impatiently. "I will accept responsibility. Come."

Hesitantly, Ozzie followed Whitley out of the inn. In truth, he was tired of sitting in the dark room with nothing to do. The last few days had been torturous. What was he doing there? What was he waiting for?

They followed the River Aare to a small café in the village. Outside, a man held a large half-round of cheese to an open fire and scraped the melted portions onto a plate.

When it was brought inside, Whitley pointed it out to the waitress who nodded and said, "Raclette." She brought them a fresh plate, along with a small wood bucket of boiled potatoes, a plate of pickles, and a bowl of pickled onions. Whitley devoured everything quite noisily while Ozzie could only pick at the melted cheese.

"My father is a stationmaster," Whitley said, his mouth full of food. "A dull man with no sense of the world. I thought working for my uncle would show me things, bring me wealth and adventure. I know his business and have accepted it. I have done all he has asked. And yet, I don't have his respect or even his attention anymore."

Ozzie studied Whitley and realized, but for the beard, he did not seem all that old — maybe eighteen or nineteen.

"I have not been involved in my uncle's organization for long, but I have done my best." Whitley paused between bites. His eyes grew glassy. "And now I am being stalked by Sherlock Holmes, no less. I should never have left Bristol."

Ozzie understood how Whitley felt. He had regrets, too, and wished he'd never left London. In spite of his best intentions, he had not helped the only friends he had ever known. He had not helped Master — the person he had come to admire above all others.

Seeing that Whitley was in a talking mood, Ozzie asked, "Did you know your uncle's wife, and his son?"

Whitley cocked his head, knit his brow, and looked quizzically at Ozzie.

Is he surprised that I know about them? Ozzie

wondered. Jealous, perhaps, that Moriarty confided in me?

"If you wish to know about my uncle," Whitley said flatly, "you'll have to learn it from someone else."

CHAPTER THIRTY-FOUR

GOING HOME
WITHOUT OZZIE

Holmes and company were met in Aarmuhle by Mycroft. He sat on the patio of a café overlooking the river, drinking a coffee, without a care in the world.

"Who's that?" Elliot asked.

From the street, Wiggins watched Master approach. Watson joined them. Master did not seem at all surprised to see Mycroft, though Watson was clearly perplexed.

Wiggins, Pilar, and the others waited across the street. "That's Master's brother." Pilar's voice was tight.

"Do you think he's sendin' us back?" Wiggins asked.

Pilar nodded grimly. "My thoughts exactly."

"I am ready to go back," Alfie said. "Spendin' so much time with adults ain't much fun."

"We can't go back without Ozzie," Pilar said matter-of-factly. Meanwhile, she strained to read Master's and Mycroft's lips. But Master's back was to her, and Watson obstructed her view of Mycroft.

In spite of doubting Ozzie's loyalty, and yearning to go home and find a new place to settle, Wiggins knew Pilar was right: They had to find Ozzie. He was their mate, Wiggins's *best* mate.

Twenty minutes later, Master, Watson, and Mycroft joined them. Master introduced his brother. As he spoke, a train steamed into the village from the east and stopped at the station.

When the whistle died down, Holmes addressed the gang. "We have traveled together long enough. Mycroft will now accompany you back to London. Your services have been valuable, but this trip has become too dangerous. There are matters I need to address alone."

"But the job is not finished, Master," Wiggins protested.

"And what about Ozzie?" Pilar added.

"We've come this far," Elliot said, not finishing his thought.

"Can't we just travel on our own?" Alfie suggested.

Holmes held up a hand and shook his head.

"Someone tried to assassinate me yesterday. It would have been a tragedy if that boulder had struck one of you. I can no longer accept the responsibility of your company. I have urged Watson to join you, but he refuses. I cannot stop my old friend from foolhardy behavior, but I can protect you from yourselves. We shall be done with this matter shortly. Then we will all meet in London, back on Baker Street once again."

Pilar and Wiggins continued to object as Master accompanied them to the train.

Sounding exasperated in a way they had not experienced before, Holmes said, "Your company poses a threat to my well-being and possibly to Osgood's. I have a mission to complete. I cannot do so if you follow."

At last, Pilar and Wiggins relented.

Mycroft boarded the train and led the Irregulars to a private compartment he had reserved. Feeling numb, Wiggins gazed out the window and watched Holmes and Watson on the platform. His chest ached.

Pilar closed her eyes and tried to picture meeting up again in London, as Master had said. But she could only conjure a hazy image in her mind — of Ozzie and Holmes — and it left her feeling afraid.

CHAPTER THIRTY-FIVE

OZZIE AND HOLMES MEET AGAIN

Ozzie, Moriarty, and Moran arrived in Meiringen from Giessbach on Monday morning. Whitley had disappeared shortly after lunch in Frutigen two days before. He had told Ozzie he wanted to go for a stroll and would meet him back at the inn, but he never reappeared.

Moriarty did not seem surprised or concerned when he returned with Moran that evening. "The boy should never have left Bristol. It doesn't matter, though. I have you and Moran." He patted Ozzie on the shoulder.

In Meiringen, they checked into the Hotel du Sauvage and were shown to their rooms. Moments later, a man dressed as a local visited. He spoke in a hushed tone to Moriarty, who handed him a bundle of francs and sent him out. Moran left shortly thereafter and returned with a package, an Alpine staff for hiking, and more news, which he shared privately with Moriarty.

All the while, Ozzie sat in silence.

After what felt like a fortnight, Moriarty addressed him. "You will meet with Holmes again . . ."

Ozzie's chest grew tight.

". . . But this time, I need you to approach him in disguise."

"Why?"

"The circumstances require it," Moriarty said flatly.

Ozzie noticed that the corners of Moriarty's mouth twitched as he spoke. Is it a sign of impatience? Ozzie wondered. Or does Moriarty not trust me? Why do I *want* him to trust me?

Moran removed from the parcel a felt hat with a silk band, a loose-fitting shirt, a leather vest with matching leather shorts, suspenders, high socks, and boots. He handed everything to Ozzie. "You will look like a traditional Swiss lad."

Moriarty placed a small actor's makeup kit on the desk and motioned for Ozzie to sit in the desk chair. Then he set to work: He widened Ozzie's nose with putty. He mixed hair tint in a washing bowl and dyed Ozzie's hair and eyebrows black. He stuffed balls of wax into Ozzie's cheeks to make them rounder and less gaunt. Smiling at the effect, he held up a small mirror for Ozzie to see himself. It was shocking how different he looked — so much so that he thought he might actually fool the master of disguise himself.

Moriarty spoke a few words in English with a Swiss-German accent and told Ozzie to imitate him.

"Excellent, Master Manning, you mimic well." Moriarty rested a hand gently on Ozzie's shoulder. "Remember, you are a Swiss lad and know only a handful of English words. Otherwise, remain silent and pretend you do not understand."

"But sir, Master — I mean Holmes — knows German. He may try to speak to me."

Moriarty scowled. "I do not care to hear of Holmes's talents. Your task is to act as a messenger and do whatever necessary to fool him. I will provide you with a letter to deliver and then you shall leave. Do not dally!" His voice was laced with venom.

Ozzie recoiled. Why is Moriarty suddenly directing his anger toward *me*?

"Yes, sir." Ozzie gave a slight bow before going to the bathroom to put on the clothes. The short trousers were stiff and uncomfortable. His pale, bony knees, which had never been exposed to the sun, stuck out unnaturally above the high socks. He looked ridiculous and suddenly felt certain that, in spite of the makeup, Master would recognize him. Ozzie lifted his staff.

Sometime after noon, Moriarty's informant reappeared and led them to a nearby hotel, the Englischer Hof. As usual, Moran carried his rucksack, which Ozzie just now realized probably contained the disassembled air gun.

The proprietor of the hotel, a Herr Steiler, informed Moriarty that Holmes and Watson had departed on foot for Rosenlaui just minutes ago and were planning a small detour to Reichenbach Falls.

Moriarty requested a piece of hotel stationery. He then proceeded to a patio on the back side of the hotel, wrote a long message, and sealed it in an envelope, which he handed to Ozzie.

"I have had enough cat and mouse. We shall soon be done with this foolish game."

Moriarty pointed to the mountain before them. "Head up that hill and follow Holmes and Watson to the falls. When you reach them, hand this message directly to Watson. Tell him it's from Herr Steiler. Once you have finished your business, continue immediately to Rosenlaui."

"What then?" Ozzie asked.

"We will meet there, you and I, to discuss your future. Would you like that?" Moriarty smiled warmly.

Ozzie felt relieved that the professor no longer seemed angry with him. Still, he said nothing and just stared back at him.

"Remember," Moriarty said, "*I* offered an accord. It was *Holmes* who declined."

Without further discussion, Ozzie set out, awkwardly moving his staff. He felt his chest constrict, from the altitude or from the experience of the last week, he was not sure. But one thing he knew for certain: He had started with a clear plan of assisting Master and capturing Moriarty — and now he no longer had any idea what he was doing. His mind still felt filled with fog; he knew it was not working right. He tried to take a deep breath, but it only made him cough. The landscape began to spin. Why had he spent so much time with Moriarty? Why hadn't he run away — to Master or back to England — when the opportunity presented itself? What did he want out of all of this? Adventure? A father?

Ozzie's chest burned. He missed his mates and wondered what Wiggins, Pilar, and the rest of the Irregulars were doing. Were they safe? Had Wiggins found a new home for them in London? Was Pilar in trouble with Madam Estrella? Apart from when his mother died, he had never felt lonelier.

He gripped the staff tightly in one hand and clutched the envelope in the other. What did the message inside say? Should he open it?

About halfway up the mountain, Ozzie turned and followed a path that led to Reichenbach Falls. The path had been cut out of the side of the mountain and became quite narrow. He stopped and peered over. There was no railing or buffer, just a hundred or more foot drop into the abyss. Ozzie stepped closer to the inside edge of the path.

He could feel his throat tense. The summits and the trees that dotted them closed in around him. He hugged the stone wall and crept along. Gradually, his nerves settled as he approached the falls.

A vast flow of white water cascaded from a high ledge and tumbled somewhere far below. Its descent formed a thick spray of mist. Though beautiful, the falls filled Ozzie with an ominous feeling. The mist blew its way back up the cliffs, chilling him and obscuring his vision.

As best he could, he followed the path around

another rock face, only to come abruptly upon Holmes and Watson. They stood a short distance from where the path ended in a sharp drop before the falls.

When they saw him, Watson seemed surprised, but Master's expression was impassive. Did they recognize him? Without a word, they met one another halfway. Ozzie offered the envelope to Watson. "From Herr Steiler," he said in his Swiss-German accent. He did not worry about the quality of it because the sound of the falls muffled his voice.

Watson read the letter and then shared its contents with Holmes: Herr Steiler urgently requested Watson's assistance with a sick Englishwoman who had just checked into the hotel. Her condition was dire, and she asked specifically for an English doctor.

"He says it is consumption, Holmes." Watson's brow furrowed. "I am hesitant to leave you . . . but the demands of my profession are such . . . well, I must go."

"Do not worry, my friend. I understand." Holmes looked at Ozzie. "I will keep this young man as my guide to Rosenlaui. You can meet me there this evening."

Suddenly it struck Ozzie — Moriarty had written the note to intentionally separate Master and Watson! Obviously, he wanted Master alone so he could strike.

Though the air was chilled, Ozzie felt his neck and arms grow hot. I am responsible for helping to trap Master, he realized. If only I had read the note, perhaps I could have devised a plan. You must do something, he urged himself. But he just stood there, frozen, as he listened to Watson agree to Holmes's instructions and watched him tip his hat and head purposefully back down the path.

"A touch of his hat . . ." Holmes sighed as he watched Watson depart. "The everyday gesture of a friend becomes significant when you suspect it may be the last time you see it. Oh, Watson! My dearest friend, how sad you will be when you realize that Moriarty has tricked you into leaving me alone."

Ozzie realized he had never heard Master speak so tenderly. *Was* he capable of affection after all?

As if reading his thoughts, Holmes turned to him. "So, Herr Manning, am I alone?" He set his staff against a boulder, leaned against the stone wall, and crossed his arms as he gazed intently into Ozzie's eyes.

Ozzie felt washed with relief, both because Master recognized him and for the chance to redeem himself. He removed the wax from his cheeks and the putty from his nose. "No, Master. I will stay with you."

"That would be a mistake. Moriarty will appear on that path sometime in the next twenty minutes. He will not be here to converse. I suggest you continue on the trail to Rosenlaui. Watson will take care of you and make certain that you get safe passage back to London."

Ozzie could hear the concern in Master's voice, as well as something else. Was it resignation? To death? It made Ozzie want to stay all the more. "The professor directed me to do the same."

"We think alike," said Master with a smirk, "just to contrary ends."

Ozzie felt paralyzed. Should he obey Master and

go? Would this be the last time he ever saw him? Would he never learn whether or not Master was his father? Desperate, he said, "But Moran is with Moriarty. You will be outnumbered."

Holmes shook his head. "This matter has become personal with Moriarty. I believe he will confront me alone. Likewise, I wish the same. Do not feel that you must prove something to me, Osgood. I have never for a moment doubted your loyalty."

"I will not leave you," Ozzie said.

Holmes reached out and put a hand on Ozzie's shoulder. "I'm afraid I must insist. I have always tried to protect you. Your presence will only distract me from my purpose. The paths we tread now are too dangerous. . . ."

Ozzie swallowed back a lump in his throat.

Holmes squeezed Ozzie's shoulder and forced him to meet his gaze. "You have wanted to ask me a question for some time. I suspect I know what it is. . . ."

Ozzie gazed back, his mind churning. All this time, Master knew?

As if reading his thoughts again, Holmes said, "You have been searching for your father for as long as we have been acquainted. Ever since you returned from your travels in Oxfordshire, you have acted differently toward me, even going so far as to share a picture of your mother with me. . . ."

Ozzie sensed the answer to the only question he ever cared about was coming. His head grew hot.

"I'm sorry, Osgood, but I have no children of my own. You are a unique young man, but you are not my son."

Ozzie felt the blood drain from his face. A shrillness echoed in his ears. Was he going to pass out?

Then, from somewhere, he had a flash of understanding. Master is saying this to make me leave! He is just trying to protect me.

Ozzie looked up into the master detective's face, and for the first time since he'd started his travels, he knew exactly what to do.

CHAPTER THIRTY-SIX

THE
FINAL MEETING

Steiler, the hotel proprietor, examined the two of them inquisitively, hesitating before he spoke. The English boy and the olive-skinned girl looked totally out of place in their strange, formal clothing. Yet they appeared innocent enough.

"Two Englishmen left earlier this morning. To the falls and then on to Rosenlaui."

Before he walked away, he added, "You are not the first to inquire. Two others were here. They left less than an hour ago with a local boy."

Wiggins and Pilar thanked him and walked out onto the back terrace of the hotel and gazed up at the mountain. Other than a lone traveler heading down the trail toward them, they could not see anyone.

"Steiler saw Master and Watson, and it sounds like Moriarty and Moran are following," Wiggins said.

Pilar nodded her agreement.

Wiggins frowned. "So where's Oz?"

Though the two had steamed off in the train with Mycroft and the others the day before, they had no intention of returning to England without Ozzie. As soon as they'd entered the train carriage, they began pleading with Mycroft to assist them in finding him. Having had no experience with strong-minded youth, Holmes's brother had succumbed to their wishes, but only after obtaining what he considered a reasonable compromise.

Wiggins and Pilar agreed that they would no longer trail Holmes or try to assist him in capturing Moriarty if they were given two more days to retrieve their friend. They all disembarked at the next stop. Reluctantly, Rohan, Elliot, and Alfie waited with Mycroft, who seemed to lack the energy to follow.

"You must tell your friend Osgood that he can no longer be of assistance. He will only suffer harm if he falls between Moriarty and my brother. This game will not end like Sherlock's others. You must impress this upon him."

Mycroft had then told Wiggins and Pilar where Holmes and Watson were headed, provided them with additional funds, and hired them a carriage.

"Ozzie must still be with them," Pilar said as she watched the figure continue down the trail toward them. "Maybe Steiler was wrong and thought Ozzie was a local boy."

Wiggins's heart began to race when he recognized the solitary traveler approaching the hotel. "It's Dr. Watson!"

They ran to him and told him what they knew. Upon hearing that Moriarty and Moran were in close pursuit, Watson quickly found Steiler. It took only a moment for him to realize that he'd been tricked; there was no sick woman at the hotel.

Immediately, Watson, Wiggins, and Pilar set out for Reichenbach Falls.

Despite his limp, Watson practically charged up the mountain, repeating under his breath, "What have I done? What have I done?"

Wiggins and Pilar exchanged anxious looks but kept quiet.

Pilar tried to picture in her mind what had happened to Ozzie. But no images came. She couldn't decide if that and the weak feeling in her stomach were simply worry, or signs of something ominous.

For his part, Wiggins could not slow his heart. Ever since he first saw Watson, it pounded in his ears with punishing persistence.

Still, he kept on, as did Pilar and Watson. They were quite winded when they reached the path that led to the falls. The dirt on the path became wetter and wetter as they walked, and soon they could make out distinct footprints.

Wiggins stopped and pointed to them. They recognized Watson's boot marks, which traveled in both directions. Three other sets of footprints were visible as well. Two sets were from larger man-size boots and the third were slightly smaller. All three sets headed down the path toward the falls. But unlike Watson's, none of them returned.

Watson gasped. Before he could say anything, Wiggins and Pilar ran down the path, barely managing to maintain their balance as it curved around the cliffs, until they reached the end. A vast chasm stretched between them and Reichenbach Falls. Here the footprints jumbled and crisscrossed, as if their bearers had engaged in some sort of wild dance, before slipping off the path and plunging over the side of the cliff.

Pilar did not need to peer down to know what had happened. She held her head and sank to her knees. "No!" she wailed, her voice swallowed by the roar of the falls.

Disbelieving, Wiggins couldn't help but look down into the chasm. Surely Master had found a way to save himself and Ozzie. But the waterfall rushed headlong, unrelenting, into the abyss. And there was not a soul in sight. Wiggins did not even feel his legs buckle, nor the cold wet ground beneath him, when he sank to the mud and howled.

In a daze, Watson lifted the master detective's staff, which was resting against a boulder, and stared at it blankly. He raised a hand to his brow and said quietly, "Holmes."

Wiggins was not sure how long they stayed that way, but eventually, Pilar took his hand and helped him to his feet. Before they headed back down the path, Wiggins took one last look at the falls. In his mind's eye, he pictured his best friend and recreated the struggle between Holmes and Moriarty. Did Ozzie ever learn whether Master was his father? Wiggins wondered.

In the end, did it matter? They had been together and Ozzie had helped Master when he needed it most.

Esteemed Reader,

Even after all these many years, I still feel the
sadness of that day at Reichenbach Falls, where I
suffered the loss of my best friend, Osgood Manning,
and my fine employer, Mr. Sherlock Holmes. Had
it not been for the strength and spirit of Miss Pilar
Ana Maria de la Vega, I might have wandered those
Swiss mountains aimlessly and wasted away.

By now, and perhaps long before now, dear
reader, you have deduced that I, Arthur Wiggins,
am the chronicler of these tales. I hope you can
forgive me for shrouding my identity in mystery
and now offering it up so casually. My intent in

remaining anonymous was simply to keep the focus on my mates, the Baker Street Irregulars.

That most horrific day at Reichenbach Falls still preys upon me. The three of us stood frozen, sick with shock and sorrow. Then Dr. Watson observed a reflection from something resting on a nearby boulder. Reaching for it, he discovered Master's cigarette case and beneath it, a note from Master. The content of that message is documented in Dr. Watson's remembrance, "The Adventure of the Final Problem." In sum, Master bid him adieu and confirmed that he anticipated fighting Moriarty to their mutual deaths. Watson could barely keep his composure as he read Master's farewell.

Our return to England was a blur. After meeting with the Swiss authorities, Pilar, Watson, and I rejoined Mycroft and the others and took an interminable train ride followed by an equally unpleasant steamer passage back to England.

As you might imagine, I returned home so distraught that my natural instincts of survival all but left me. Without Pilar and her kind, wise mother, Madam Estrella, I daresay I might not be here to tell this tale.

I am afraid the Irregulars as a gang began to dissolve even before our return to London. On the steamer crossing back to England, Rohan so impressed the first mate with his knowledge of ships that he was offered a position as a cabin boy. Out of loyalty, Rohan waited a few weeks after we returned home before he accepted the position.

The Bloomfields agreed to house some of us in return for our labor, or to place us with other farmers and businesses in the area.

To my surprise, Elliot stayed with the Bloomfields, along with Barnaby and Shem. The others were hired out to nearby farms. They had grown comfortable with regular meals and clean beds and were ready to give up scavenging for food and sleeping on a cold, damp floor. Only Alfie rejected country life. In his words, it was "dull as three-day-old gruel."

Heavyhearted, I returned to London with Alfie, and we spent the next several months sleeping on the floor of Madam Estrella's sitting room. During the day, I wandered London's streets looking for new accommodations, all the while wondering what to do with myself. In spite of Alfie's attempts to cheer me, and Pilar's empathy (for she was still in mourning, too), I felt lost. Without work or my own place, without the Irregulars and Master and Ozzie, I lacked a purpose. At the tender age of twelve, I thought my life was over.

And then one morning, two months after we had returned from Switzerland, I received a note from Mycroft Holmes. He asked me to meet him and stressed that I come alone. Intrigued, I swiftly readied myself. Fortunately, Alfie had wandered down to the Thames, and Pilar was busy with her studies. And so I set out for Pall Mall that afternoon unaccompanied.

It was an oppressive summer day in London, and I had sweated through my shirt by the time I reached the Diogenes Club.

I climbed the grand stone steps and was shown to Mycroft's private chamber. As I passed through the club, I could not help but notice how silently its members treaded through the halls and turned away from me and one another. A very unsocial group, those men of the Diogenes.

Mycroft's rooms were dark and cool, though some light seeped through the leaded-glass windows. Mycroft sat in a black leather chair, with his feet resting on a matching ottoman. He fluttered a small Chinese fan before his face and smiled up at me.

"I have only begun to recover from the exertions of our travels on the Continent." His expression seemed to suggest that I had not.

He continued in a businesslike manner. "I have been directed to provide you with some information, though I have also been told to exercise my discretion in doing so." Mycroft studied me intensely, as if trying to see into my soul. While he did so, I noticed on the smoking table beside his chair a small brown envelope. It did not take great skills of deduction to realize that was the subject of our meeting.

After what seemed like an eternal pause, Mycroft cleared his throat. "I am sure in your dealings with my brother, Sherlock, you have been asked to keep matters confidential. None of the information you have previously protected compares with what I shall now share with you." Mycroft lifted the envelope and handed it to me. My name appeared in block letters on the front.

"The information inside is not to be shared with your friends, nor with Dr. Watson. You must guard the contents until the deaths of all those involved." He then nodded for me to open it.

I tore open the envelope and immediately recognized the handwriting. For the first time in months, I felt my heart beat with excitement.

With the basic reading skills Ozzie had taught me and some assistance from Mycroft, I read the letter, which was dated approximately one month prior.

My dear friend Wiggins,

I hope you can forgive my long silence, but Master has insisted that we keep our survival secret. It is only after weeks of ratio-nal discussion that I convinced him of the importance of telling you the truth. We both have the utmost confidence in your discretion.

Ecstatic, I stopped reading. I wanted to scream or dance! "They're alive?!" I whispered incredulously. Mycroft smiled and nodded. I continued reading.

As you can plainly tell, we did not perish at Reichenbach Falls; only Professor Moriarty met his end. I will explain what I can, but let me start with the days leading up to the final meeting.

My time with Moriarty was strange. The professor had a hold on me in ways I am only beginning to understand. I believe he sensed my need for a father, and manipulated me. But you must know, I never once lost my loyalty to Master or the Irregulars.

Here Ozzie summarized his last days with Moriarty, which I have already documented in my own words in the earlier chapters of this adventure. The letter continued.

Upon seeing Master face-to-face by the falls, all conflicting feelings left me. Master, for all his lack of emotion and attention, possesses an honesty and clarity of purpose that washed away any softness I felt toward the professor. Ironically, the very emotions that had led me astray showed me why Master avoided such human tendencies.

On that fateful day at Reichenbach Falls, Master insisted that I leave him so that he could face Moriarty alone. Out of blind stubbornness and loyalty, I refused. I also wanted the professor to know that his powers over me had failed and that I stood by Master.

Moriarty soon appeared on the path alone just as Master had said he would. His attention was solely on Master; I seemed to no longer exist to him. Now I see that he anticipated my allegiance even before I understood it.

The two men exchanged a few words and headed down toward the end of the trail as if setting out for some sporting match. I followed Master, and Moriarty trailed us. Just as we reached the end of the path, I felt the claws of Moriarty seize my shoulders, and he lifted me off my feet. He dropped me at the edge of the cliff and leaned me out over the chasm.

Moriarty stared at Master as he held me.

If I had any doubts that I was the professor's pawn, all of it was erased at that moment. I could hardly breathe.

Master looked coolly into Moriarty's eyes and said, "That will change nothing." With lightning speed, Master grabbed me and swung me onto the trail. Seeing Master off balance, Moriarty clutched him around the waist from behind and squeezed him tightly with his arms. Master groaned and his arms flailed above his head as Moriarty spun him toward the edge.

I would like to say that I had the presence

of mind to jump to my feet and assist Master, but I froze. After all their brain work, after all their calculation, there teetered two of the greatest minds of the time, entwined, rocking to and fro in a primal dance. I was sure of their mutual destruction.

But suddenly, Master's legs gained purchase and, with a shrug of his whole body, he broke free of Moriarty's grasp. Then, with a swift and fluid sweep of his arms, he heaved Moriarty into the abyss.

Arms flapping and legs kicking, the professor tumbled through the air. A high-pitched wail echoed from the chasm as Moriarty crashed into a lower cliff and his body disappeared into the mist.

I crouched on the side of the trail, holding my stomach. I had never before seen somebody die.

Without a word, Master lifted me to my feet and directed me to walk backward toward the stone boulders that bordered the path. He did the same. He then boosted me up to a ledge hardly visible from the path and pulled himself after me. He motioned for me to remain silent, and we crouched down and waited.

A few minutes later, you, Pilar, and Dr. Watson appeared. Master signaled me to keep quiet. We watched you study our footprints on the trail, drawing of course the wrong conclusion. I felt miserable watching you and Pilar mourn me, but Master's firm grip on my arm told me he had a plan.

After the three of you left for Meiringen, we did not dally. Master continued to climb across the face of the cliff and I followed. The climbing was tricky, for there were few handholds and footholds. I was sure I would fall. Finally, we reached another ledge and rested, only to be startled by the sound of a man's voice just above us on the mountain. When we looked up, Moran was banging his air gun on the ground and swearing. That's when I remembered disabling the gun's pump back in Paris. Before I could explain to

Master what had happened, a boulder came bounding down and crashed a few feet away from us. A minute later, Moran hurled a second rock within inches of Master's head.

Master grabbed my elbow and led me off the ledge. Because of the steepness of the cliff, we could not see the trail below us. Master pulled me along until we both began to slide some twenty feet down a jagged stone face and then fell another ten feet onto the trail. Our clothes tore and we both got bloodied. Climbing to his feet, Master began to run, pausing for a moment to wave me on. We must have gone ten miles that afternoon and evening before we stopped on the outskirts of a small village and took refuge in a hayrick.

We had barely spoken a word until then. I had so many questions. Why had we run away? Why did we allow our dearest friends to think that we were dead?

Master explained.

"I have decided to take a sabbatical. With Moriarty's demise, I fear the business of detection will not be the same. While there are a few dregs who will attempt to avenge him, they no longer pose any significant threat to society. My services are not needed as they once were. Moran knows we are alive, but he will not share this fact because doing so would reveal that he failed in his attempt to kill me. Still, he may seek revenge on me. So I must disappear. We must make it seem that I did not survive my confrontation with Moriarty. I am afraid that includes keeping my survival a secret even from my friend and biographer, Watson."

By then, night had fallen. We rested in the hay in total darkness as I considered all that he had said. Though sad and weary, some part of me found our adventure that day exhilarating. Master and I were traveling together with a common purpose. This was what I had always wanted.

"I have other interests I wish to pursue," Master continued. "To satisfy them, I will travel the world. But there is one problem:

what to do with you, Osgood. I did not plan for your presence."

We sat in silence for some time. In my mind, the answer was simple: Take me with you. Before I could answer, Master said, "You certainly cannot return to England or remain on the Continent, for you would be too easily discovered. For now, I suppose you must join me, Osgood."

I grinned in the darkness.

The next morning, we continued our journey. I cannot share with you our path, but within two weeks we were on our way to the Orient.

Each day, we travel together. For how much longer, I cannot say. There has been talk of me attending boarding school somewhere. Who knows what may happen. For now, I feel happy. Though Master is not my father, he provides for me and treats me with kindness and respect. What more could I hope for?

And Wiggins, what I have seen of the world! I thought the end of my time with *the Irregulars and our work as detectives would be the end of great adventures. How wrong I have been! Pilar, who traveled so much, as a young girl, knew a truth that we had yet to learn. There are new worlds to explore, new people to experience, new adventures waiting. Wiggins, with all your ingenuity, you must discover them, for I am beginning to see that it is the key to everything.*

I do wish I were making such discoveries with you. I am afraid it may be a long time before I see you again. But I give you my word that I will. Until then, please always remember that I remain,

Your Best Friend.

Sincerely,

Osgood Manning

When I finished the letter, my hands were shaking. I looked up at Mycroft, who was smiling and still waving the fan.

"I believe my brother and your friend thought

it important for you to know the truth of the situation so that you may continue on with your life. What they shared with you could compromise their very existence. Remember, it is your obligation to keep the secret and also to move on and live."

I nodded and thanked Mycroft. Then I left and walked through London for the rest of the day and into the night, thinking about Ozzie and all that he had said. By the time I returned to Pilar's flat, the sun had begun to rise again. I felt burdened by the information I had to keep from Pilar and Alfie and the others. At the same time, I knew I must do something to pay homage to some of the best and most important years of my life. But what?

Many of the years that followed were not easy. Thankfully, Pilar and I remained the closest of friends, even when she moved to Madrid, and even when she learned much later that Ozzie was still alive and that I had known all along. But that is another story.

In those early years, Alfie and I continued to live together, and I looked after him, which gave me a sense of purpose. Still, there were times when I thought I would fail. But Ozzie's words inspired me, and my old resilience returned and sustained me.

Eventually, I found my way into business and became quite successful. But my greatest pride is the home I opened in a converted carriage factory, for street urchins like myself. Hope that they might be given opportunities, such as Sherlock Holmes gave me and my mates.

I am old now, and much time has passed. There were so many adventures I have not had time to share. They, too, were grand. Still, when I look back, I wonder if any of them compares to those days with Sherlock Holmes and the Baker Street Irregulars.

Thank you for traveling with us.

Respectfully yours,
Sir Arthur Wiggins
London, England
1955

FACTS and PRACTICALS
for the
ASPIRING DETECTIVE

SLANG GLOSSARY

Bees and honey: money (page 2)

Burke: stupid person (page 4)

China (short for china plate): mate (page 9)

Duckin' and divin': skiving, or evading work (page 23)

Sugar and honey: money (page 24)

Collywobbles: creeps (page 25)

Pen and ink: stink (page 25)

Groat: money (page 38)

Rabbit (short for rabbit and pork): talk (page 66)

Loaf (short for bread loaf): head (page 76)

Butcher's (short for butcher's hook): look (page 90)

Spotted (short for spotted dick, a dessert): sick (page 123)

DEMYSTIFYING THE MYSTERY

If you have read to the end of this quartet, you are on your way to becoming a seasoned mystery reader. By now, you know firsthand that mysteries not only make for riveting reading, they are also beneficial to the brain! Giving the old cerebellum a workout with deduction will surely increase the gray matter and make you a more nimble thinker. As Sherlock Holmes says, "I never remember feeling tired by work, but idleness exhausts me completely."

Have you noticed that within this tantalizing genre, there are different types of mysteries? Each one employs its own tricks to tempt the reader into trying to solve the story's puzzle. Following is a sampling of the various subgenres.

Whodunit? In this classic mystery format, the crime is presented up front. As the story unfolds, suspects emerge and the reader tries to determine who the perpetrator is.

How Was It Done? In this scenario, the reader knows or suspects who the architect of the crime is, but must figure out how the crime was done and how to prove it.

Can You Stop It? Here the crime is about to happen and the perpetrator may even be known. The trick is to determine how to prevent the crime from taking place.

Sometimes, more than one subgenre is used in a single story. Can you figure out which ones are used in each of the Sherlock Holmes and the Baker Street Irregulars books?

Now that you are well versed in the genre, why not try your hand at writing your own mystery?!

TRAINS IN VICTORIAN TIMES

Trains revolutionized nineteenth-century England and featured prominently in the expansion of industry, communications, and culture in the Victorian era. The first train lines in England were constructed shortly before the coronation of Queen Victoria in 1837 and spread quickly throughout the country in the coming decades. By the time the Baker Street Irregulars assisted Sherlock Holmes in his cases, trains connected every major city and many small ones.

Trains created new businesses and provided greater opportunities for the English people. For example, raw materials such as iron or coal could be hauled by freight trains in greater quantities and at faster speeds than ever before, which allowed for production in more locales. Perishable goods such as fish or dairy could be sent to city markets from much greater distances, offering greater variety and nutrition in people's diets.

The speed of trains allowed people to travel greater distances for their work. As a result, suburbs began to develop outside of cities and people commuted to their jobs.

Trains of the Victorian era were pulled by steam engines. The passenger trains had first-, second-, and sometimes third-class cars, which were priced based upon luxury and comfort. First-class cars had leather seats and carpets; third-class cars often had no seats. Trains that traveled long distances sometimes had dining cars and specially designed cars for sleeping called Pullman cars.

By an act of Parliament, all the railroads were required to have one train a day that would stop at each station along its entire line and charge no more than a penny a mile. These "parliamentary trains" allowed the poor to take advantage of the speed convenience of train travel.

Of course, there were some shortcomings to train travel. Accidents were common. Steam engines did not burn fuel cleanly. And trains did not have bathrooms. Yet, trains affected almost every aspect of Victorian society, and peoples' daily lives improved because of them.

ARE YOU A SHERLOCKIAN OR A DOYLEIAN?

The world of Sherlock Holmes fans and scholars falls into two primary groups — Sherlockians and Doyleians.

Doyleians believe that Sherlock Holmes is the fictional creation of the writer Sir Arthur Conan Doyle.

Sherlockians believe that Sherlock Holmes is a real living master detective whose cases were documented by his friend and biographer Dr. John Watson and who was assisted in those cases by a band of loyal street urchins — the Baker Street Irregulars.

To them, Sir Arthur Conan Doyle, though an

excellent writer, physician, and patriot, acted solely as a literary agent for Dr. Watson.

What do you believe?

SIR ARTHUR CONAN DOYLE

A SHORT BIOGRAPHY

Arthur Ignatius Conan Doyle was born in Edinburgh, Scotland, in 1859. As a boy, his mother, Mary, a gifted storyteller, entertained him with stories from books as well as those of her own creation. Her stories were often based upon the deeds of knights and other gallant folk. In addition to listening to stories, young Arthur also enjoyed athletics, favoring cricket, and remained a sports enthusiast his entire life.

He attended the University of Edinburgh, where he studied medicine and had his first stories published. One of his medical professors was a man named Dr. Joseph Bell, who had amazing analytical skills. Dr. Bell was said to have the ability to deduce the occupation of a person just by physically examining him. It is believed that Dr. Bell's abilities so impressed Arthur Conan Doyle that he used them as the basis for the character Sherlock Holmes.

In 1887, Arthur Conan Doyle, now a practicing physician, published his first Sherlock Holmes story. The novel, *A Study in Scarlet*, appeared in the magazine *Beeton's Christmas Annual*. Conan Doyle proceeded to write and publish fifty-six short stories and three more novels featuring Sherlock Holmes. He dedicated his collection of stories, *The Adventures of Sherlock Holmes*, to Dr. Bell.

Though Conan Doyle wrote other works of fiction and nonfiction, he remains best known for Sherlock Holmes, whom many people consider the most widely recognized character in all literature worldwide.